TO: Rosie,

Thanks you for the support

Rosco

DEATH'S

VALLEY

A Novel

Roy A. Teel Jr.

DEATH'S VALLEY

A Novel

Roy A. Teel Jr.

The Iron Eagle Series: Book Seven

An Imprint of Narroway Publishing LLC.

Narroway Publishing LLC.
Imprint: Narroway Press
P.O. Box 1431
Lake Arrowhead, California 92352

This is a work of fiction. Names, characters, places, and incidents either are the product of the author's imagination or are used fictitiously, and any resemblance to actual persons, living or dead, business establishments, events or locales is entirely coincidental.

First Edition

ISBN: 978-0-9903637-7-4

Teel, Roy A., 1965-
    Death's Valley: A Novel, The Iron Eagle Series: Book Seven /
    Roy A. Teel Jr. — 1st ed. — Lake Arrowhead, Calif. Narroway Press
    c2015. p. ; cm. ISBN: 978-0-9903637-7-4 (Hardcover)

1. Hard-Boiled – Fiction. 2. Police, FBI – Fiction. 3. Murder – Fiction.
4. Serial Killers – Fiction. 5. Mystery – Fiction. 6. Suspense – Fiction.
7. Graphic Violence – Fiction. 8. Graphic Sex – Fiction.
I. Title.

    Book Editing: Finesse Writing and Editing LLC.
    Cover and Book Design: Adan M. Garcia, FSi studio
    Author Photo: F. E. Arnest

For: Frank Serpico

For his courage and strength

Also by Roy A. Teel Jr.

Nonfiction:

*The Way, The Truth, and The Lies: How the Gospels
Mislead Christians about Jesus' True Message*

*Against the Grain: The American Mega-church
and its Culture of Control*

Fiction:

The Light of Darkness: Dialogues in Death: Collected Short Stories

And God Laughed, A Novel

Fiction Novel Series:

Rise of the Iron Eagle: Book One

Evil and the Details: Book Two

Rome Is Burning: Book Three

Operation Red Alert: Book Four

A Model for Murder: Book Five

Devil's Chair: Book Six

"Corruption is like a ball of snow, once it's set a rolling it must increase."

— Charles Caleb Colton

"An honest cop still can't find a place to go and complain without fear of recrimination. The blue wall will always be there because the system supports it."

— Frank Serpico

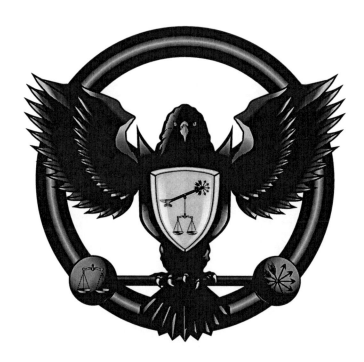

SEAL OF THE IRON EAGLE ®

Table of Contents

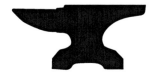

CHAPTER ONE

"You will be respectful. You understand
me, you slant-eyed piece of shit?"

It was just before sunset as John Swenson packed the last of his things to go home for the evening. He was excited because he and Sara were getting ready to take their first vacation since getting married nearly three years earlier. His secretary, Samantha Ross, walked into the office and said, "I can't believe that you're really going to leave your post for two whole weeks." "Yea, well, I won't believe it until I'm sitting on our private jet, and we are on our way." "Well, I'm going to miss you." John smiled and said, "Thanks, Sam. You'll be fine. Besides, you have to deal with Agent Owens. He will be running things in my absence." Sam frowned. "He's so damned grouchy. It's hard to work for him." John half laughed and said, "Well, Owens has been here at the Bureau for a long time. He might be grouchy, but he's a great investigator and manager." She nodded weakly and walked over and gave him a hug. At four foot ten, she was tiny next to John's huge frame. He put an arm around her and said, "I will see you in two weeks. I doubt the world is going to come to an

end while I'm gone." Sam started walking out of John's office and said, "With all the shit I've seen in the last four years working here, I wouldn't rule it out." John laughed as she disappeared into the outer office.

Steve rolled up to John's office in his wheelchair and asked, "So, you're really doing it? You're really going on vacation?" John nodded and said, "Um...so are you and Gail. Are you two packed and ready to go?" Steve looked on and said, "Yea. Gail has been packed for a week. I really feel bad that we are crashing your vacation." "You're not crashing anything. You and Gail need some time away together, and Sara is your doctor. She made it clear that she will only vacation if she has her number one patient with her." Steve smiled and said, "You're both such good people, John. This means the world to Gail and me." John shrugged and said, "I don't know how good a people we are, but we care for you and Gail...now let's get the hell out of here before something comes up that pulls us away." Steve nodded, John threw the bag over his shoulder, and the two men headed for the elevator.

John pressed the button, and when the doors opened, Jim O'Brian was standing in the elevator ready to exit. Steve looked at him and said, "No...no mother fuckin' way...John and I are gone. You didn't see us. Whatever the fuck it is, take it to Jared." Jim laughed and said, "Jared? Are you fuckin' kidding me? That guy couldn't investigate his way out of a paper bag. I'm sorry, guys. I just need a few minutes of your time, and you can be off." John slouched and took the bag off his shoulder and pushed Steve back to a conference room, and all three men entered, and Jim shut the door.

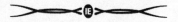

Garrison Cantrell was sitting in a holding cell at men's central jail in downtown LA waiting for his attorney to try to get him released. He had been arrested and charged with the murder of Mary Schultz. He was in holding awaiting his arraignment and was being held without bond. His attorney arrived and after being given a hard time

by other officers for defending a cop killer, he made his way to the holding room. Garrison sat silent when Ben Santone walked in. "We have the hearing, Garrison. You're pleading not guilty." Garrison nodded, and Ben said, "You know there is no way that I'm going to be able to get a bail amount set for you, right?" He nodded and said, "I'm aware. I also know that I will never make it anywhere near trial. These guys are going to kill me." Ben looked down at the table in the small room and said, "I'm going to make a motion to have you remanded to federal custody while awaiting trial. Based on what you have been telling me, I agree that you are most likely going to have an 'accident' and die or be another 'jail suicide.'" "What do you think the odds are that you can get the judge to approve it?" "Good, very, very good. The judge doesn't want your blood on her hands. I have spoken to her in chambers, and she has agreed, off the record, that you would be better off out of LAPD's jail." Ben stood up and said, "Well, time to go." Garrison stood up and looked at Ben and said, "You and I both know that I'm going down for this, and there is nothing we can do to stop it." Ben said, "There is no evidence that you did anything wrong. The case is a poorly built house of cards based on circumstantial evidence. I believe that we will prevail, and you will be acquitted." Garrison smiled weakly and said, "You are ever the optimist, Ben." He looked at Garrison and said, "No...I have never asked you about your guilt or innocence here. I know you. You're a good man, and you were a good cop. I know you had nothing to do with Schultz's death, and I'm going to show you that the system works." Garrison laughed and said, "If it does, it will be the first time." Two sheriff's deputies walked in and cuffed and shackled Garrison, and the two men headed for the Los Angeles County Superior Court where Garrison would be held for his hearing the next morning.

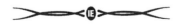

Los Angeles Police Detective Mario Sanchez had pulled up and parked outside a small market in Koreatown at the corner of West Third and Vermont Avenue. The area was bustling with strip malls and other buildings on all four corners. Sanchez walked across the parking lot, getting bumped and shoved by shoppers and tourists that had come down to the area to sightsee and shop for their daily goods. As Sanchez was nearing the entrance to the Koreatown Market, a large Hispanic man ran into him, excused himself, and then handed him a flyer. Sanchez went to throw it down on the ground but caught the disapproving eye of the man who handed it to him, so he put it inside the flap of his suit coat and pushed on into the store and straight through to the back.

He had shown up announced, and three men sat in chairs in the small, smoke-filled room with a cash counting machine that was running hundred dollar bills through it, then bundling and wrapping them in bank note paper in stacks of ten thousand dollars each.

Kim Sung, the owner of the store, saw Sanchez enter but didn't move. Sanchez pulled a chair out from the table and sat down. "So, you guys had a very good take. I see your girls have been working hard, and the illegal fight betting has been good as well as your other endeavors." There was a small, brown, brick-shaped object next him on the corner of the table, and Sanchez took out a penknife and stuck it into the side of the brick. The blade came out with a fine white powder on it. He took some on his finger and ran it across his gums. "Oh…now that's what I'm talking about. What the fuck do you cut this shit with? It's some of the best coke I have ever used," Sanchez asked, picking up a pack of bills and fanning through them.

Sung said nothing but stood up, walked over to a nearby table, pulled a bag off of it, and handed it to Sanchez. Sanchez opened it and pulled out a piece of paper. It was an accounting sheet showing the gross take from the activities that went on in the small Los Angeles enclave. "Well, I must say, you had a very, very good weekend," Sanchez said, looking into the bag and counting the cash bundled within. "Listen, gentlemen," Sanchez said, "in order to keep your police protection, we are increasing our 'fees.'" There was silence as the counting went on with no one speaking.

Sanchez continued, "I mean, you guys, of all people, understand that overhead is expensive, and we have taken on two other officers, who have agreed to provide you protection from their street cruisers. That costs us money, and I don't want to lose my cut of this deal or give up my profit. So, we are raising our fee to twenty percent. Any arguments?" There was no change in the room as the money was counted.

Sung grabbed the accounting document from Sanchez's hand and pulled an additional ten percent from the pile of cash. He handed the money to Sanchez and said, "You go now!" Sanchez sat back and said, "Hey…I'm on a break. I will watch for a few minutes. You got a problem with that?" Sung looked on, and Sanchez took the back of his hand and smacked Sung on the side of the face, knocking him out of his chair. Sanchez got up and began kicking Sung in the stomach and groin all the while saying, "You…will… not…disrespect my authority. If I had my way, you slant-eyed assholes would be in jail or deported. Actually, I would love to fuckin' blow your heads off...that's just me talking, but then there are LAWS! You are a great profit center for me and other officers, so we let you operate."

Sanchez was dripping with sweat as Sung cowered on the ground, wheezing and trying to breathe as blood was running down his face and mouth. Sanchez took a towel off the table, dried his face, and said, "Damn, Sung. It sounds like you have some broken ribs there." Sanchez kicked him hard in the chest again and asked, "Now, how do you show your gratitude for my kindness?"

Sung was in the fetal position on the ground. Sanchez grabbed him by the hair and smashed his head into the concrete floor. Sanchez unzipped his pants, pulled out his penis, and pissed all over Sung's face and upper body. Sanchez was out of breath but said as he was zipping up, "You will be respectful. You understand me, you slant-eyed piece of shit? We have gone to great lengths to get cops off the streets that would have ratted you out." He finished fixing his pants, grabbed the bag and the extra cash that had been set aside, then grabbed another hundred thousand and said, "This," he showed the cash to the men, "is a penalty for your rudeness." With that last statement, he stormed out of the store.

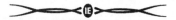

Sanchez appeared outside approximately twenty minutes after first entering the store. With the bag in his hands, he leaned on his car and lit a cigarette. The crosshairs of the sniper rifle had a perfect lock on Sanchez's head. The shooter laid flat on the smooth rooftop of the building across the street, a phone lifted to his ear, and pressed speed dial on his cell phone. "911. What is your emergency?" The voice that responded was understandable but electronic. It was a computer-generated voice used by disabled people who are unable to speak. The caller said, "There is an officer down at the corner of West Third and Vermont Avenue in the parking lot of the Koreatown Market. There are also many injured inside." The caller kept the line open as Sanchez's head bobbed slightly in the crosshairs of the rifle sight. The shooter gently squeezed the trigger, and Sanchez's head exploded like a watermelon from the force of the shot, sending brain and skull fragments in all directions. No one else was injured, and no one heard a thing.

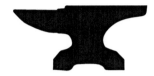

CHAPTER TWO

*"His head exploded. We don't need a
body bag...we need a sponge."*

When Jim's cell phone rang he was in the middle of reading a
report with John and Steve, and he jumped. John laughed,
as did Steve. Jim grabbed his phone and said, "WHAT THE
FUCK?" He listened, looking at John and Steve, and replied, "I'm
en route. Nobody does anything until I'm on scene." He hung up the
phone and said, "Your vacation will have to wait a few more hours. We
have a situation in Koreatown." Steve shrugged and asked, "We? Do
you have a fuckin' mouse in your pocket? John and I are on vacation!"
Jim stood up and started for the door, "Not anymore. Follow me. The
ante has just been upped in the Death's Valley murder." John and Jim
looked at each other and then followed Jim out of the building. John
and Steve jumped into John's truck, and Jim took off in his cruiser, and
off they went down Wilshire Boulevard headed for the crime scene.

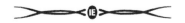

Jade Morgan was yelling instructions to police, her staff, and onlookers. "Hey, you, Mr. Policeman, do your fuckin' job! Keep those people back. Hey!" She was pointing to three members of her CSI team, "are you on the fuckin' job, or are you three here for lunch? Lock off the scene. Get this thing taped off." She was still yelling at people when John, Jim, and Steve pulled up. She saw John helping Steve out of the truck and into his wheelchair and Jim walking toward her. She cried out, "Thank God! Some real fuckin' cops. Jim, can you get some of your deputies on scene? LAPD here is ignoring me, and I'm getting pissed off. John, call your CSI team. Oh, and you're going to want to put on booties and gloves before you go anywhere near the body." John pulled his cell as did Jim, and in minutes the scene was crawling with FBI and sheriff's investigators. John walked over to Jade who was standing outside the crime scene tape and asked, "What you got?" "LAPD detective with a head shot." "Okay, so the guy was shot in the head. Let's go look at the wound." Jade looked at Jim who was standing off to the side smoking a cigarette. She walked over to him and grabbed the pack from Jim's left top pocket and took a cigarette from the pack. Jim handed her his Zippo, and she lit the cigarette with a shaky hand. John and Steve simultaneously said, "I didn't know you smoked!" She took a hit of the smoke and said coughing as she breathed out, "I gave it up ten years ago. I sneak one every now and then, and this is one of those situations." Jim asked Jade while putting the cigarettes back in his pocket, "What's the big deal? You got a head shot on a cop. Let's take a look. He's under the tarp over there, right?" Jim was pointing off in the distance.

Jade took a hit off the smoke and said, "Yep…his body is." They all three looked at each other with a puzzled look on their faces. "You said he had a head shot," John said. Jade nodded. "Then his head is under the tarp, too?" Jade shook her head. Jim said, "What the fuck? Is the guy head shot or not?" "His head exploded. We don't need a body bag to clean it up. We need a sponge." John laughed in spite of himself, walked under the crime scene tape, and lifted the tarp. Steve and Jim watched from a distance as John and Jade spoke. After about five minutes, two members of John and

Steve's team came over and said, "Sirs, you and Agent Swenson need to come into the store. You're not going to believe what we found."

Steve nodded and waved John and Jade back over; she still had the smoke between her fingers, and Steve asked, "So, what?" "Sniper." Steve and Jim looked on as Jim asked, "As in professional hit kind of sniper?" John nodded. John had a piece of paper in his gloved hand, and Jim asked, "What's that?" pointing to the paper. John said, "A list." "A list of what?" "It's not of what; it's of whom." Steve and Jim looked on, confused. John's agent was standing patiently waiting until he interrupted and said, "You three need to come into the store." Steve got an evidence bag from Jade, and he dropped the document into it, sealed the bag, and put it in his jacket pocket. Jade looked at him and said, "You're removing evidence from a crime scene?"

John frowned. "Give me a damn chain of custody form." She handed one to him, and he signed off on it and asked Jade to fill in what it was. The three men went into the location, and their agent led them into the store. There, in the back, were money counting machines, cash, and drugs. What looked like a walk-in cooler was open in the back of the room. John asked, "What's in there?" The agent started to walk them to the door while telling them that the whole building had once been a huge chain store that had gone out of business. They walked through the door to find a huge warehouse building full of beds with young women and girls in different levels of nudity, huddled in a corner with paramedics and others. Steve said, "Human trafficking?" The agent nodded, and John told him to go on about his duties as Jim and Steve made their way through the expanse of the store.

It was massive and set up like part hotel part sweatshop. They had different areas set up for sex acts from the most mundane to the most sadistic and cruel. It was all forced labor, and there were both men and women. Steve and Jim were whispering to each other as John looked on. He walked over and asked, "What are you two gabbing about?" Steve said, "The place reminds me of a place I know where a guy extracts vengeance for the greater good." John had a blank look on his face. Jim whispered,

"The lair of the Iron fuckin' Eagle!" John just shook his head and said, "Not even remotely close." The men finished looking around and went back out to the front of the store. It was nearly six p.m., and John looked at his watch and pulled the evidence bag out of his jacket pocket and said, "We need to take this back to my office and the lab." Jim and Steve asked why. John said, "The paper that Jade got off the victim is a list." Jim smarted off, "A list of what?" "A list of cops that this killer is going after."

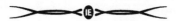

It was just before seven a.m., and Officer Marco Estrada was working street duty in his cruiser in East Los Angeles. He had been directed to work the streets and to pick up what intel he could on the movements of the Mexican Mafia. The killing of Alberto Alverez three months earlier had left unrest in the community. Even though the police commission and internal affairs blamed Alverez's death on excessive use of force and fired the officer responsible for the shooting, things were still tense. To add fuel to the fire, Alverez was a well-known gang member and the head of one of the largest drug cartels in the United States. Many didn't believe that Alverez was really dead. Conspiracy theories abounded throughout the community that it wasn't Alverez who was killed. To add even more to that was the closed casket funeral for Alverez, due to the fact that he was shot in the face with a shotgun at point-blank range.

Estrada was trying to get as much information as he could from his sources on the streets. He pulled his police cruiser into the parking lot of a seven-eleven at the corner of Whittier Boulevard and South Arizona Avenue. He walked into the twenty-four hour convenience store. The owner, Abdul Zahir, was standing behind the counter when Marco walked in, and he was greeted with a smile and a warm welcome. "How are you doing this evening, Officer Estrada?" Abdul asked in his thick Saudi Arabian accent. "Good, good, Abdul. And you?" "Very well, sir, very well." Estrada looked around the store. There were several shoppers staring him down. A small group of

young bangers were off in the corner by a fountain drink dispenser pointing at him and flashing gang symbols in his direction.

Marco looked at them and smiled then laughed. Abdul began to slink down behind the counter. Marco looked over and saw it and asked, "What are you doing?" "I don't want trouble in my store. You know they are looking for any reason to start a riot." Marco laughed and said, "Relax, Abdul. I know those kids. They ran with Alverez and his group. They're out of work right now. Besides, they don't want to mess with a cop." Abdul stood back up, and he looked on at Marco and said, "I guess that's true. You are a big intimidating officer." Marco laughed out loud and walked back to where the bangers were hanging.

He spotted nine millimeters in the waistbands of two of the five guys. He walked over to them and slapped one of them on the side of the head, pulling the weapon from his waistband. "What…the fuck…are you…thinking?" Marco held it in the air and then pointed it at the kid. There were a few tense moments, and he handed the gun back. Abdul saw the whole exchange and had a confused look on his face.

Marco said, "A fuckin' toy gun…you guys get killed over these fuckers every day. What the fuck are you thinking?" The kid held the gun in his hand and said, "We's on the street, man…we got to have our reps, man…it's all good…they don't fucks with me. I don't fucks with them." Marco shook his head and pulled his Glock from its holster and pointed it at the five. "And I can kill all of you right here, right now, and there won't even be a question. You're armed. It makes no difference if the weapon is real or not…I can't tell…I shoot first, ask questions later." "Yea, but you a Mexican like us. You won't shoot."

Marco shook his head, holstering his gun. "That's because I know you thugs, but whitey, nigger, and chink cops don't see you like me…one of them walks in or sees you on the street…BANG!… you're dead!" There was a moment of silence as they realized what was just said. "What you want, man?" one of the other kids rattled off. "Who's taking over for Alberto?" "No word." "Bullshit…don't

fuck with me. I'm a Mexican with a badge and a bad attitude, and you're five well-known banger thugs toting weapons…"

Marco put his hand on his weapon. The tone became serious, and Abdul, while he could not hear the conversation, could tell by the looks on the kids' faces that Marco had said something serious. Marco had his back to Abdul as well as the front door. The chime on the store door rang, and Marco kept his back to it, staring at the kids. All of them were wearing sunglasses, and Marco could see the reflection of the man who came in in them. He didn't move. His hand was still on his weapon when he said, "Well…hello…Andre." The kids waited for their next instructions. Andre Espinoza was second in command to Alverez, and Marco knew he was packing.

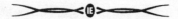

Steve and John beat Jim back to the federal building on Wilshire. John helped Steve, and the two men made their way into the building before hearing Jim screaming at the top of his lungs in a security line at the building entrance. "I'm the goddamned Sheriff of Los Angeles fuckin' County. Why is it that every time I come to this mother fuckin' building I'm treated like the local rabble?" Steve called out and said, "For God's sake, men, let the Sheriff through. He's not going to shoot up the damn place." Jim pushed his way through the metal detectors, setting them off and wreaking havoc on the system.

John and Steve were by a bank of elevators and before Jim could say another word John said, "Just shut up!" Jim was silent as they entered the elevator, and Steve took them to the top floor of the building where inmates were processed and personnel were given IDs. John walked across the hall from the elevator without saying a word, and Jim went to follow him, but Steve put his hand on Jim's arm to stop him. He looked up at Jim and said, "Just wait." John disappeared behind two dark glass unmarked doors and five minutes later emerged with something in his hand. He was walking in an angry and deliberate way as he approached them.

John reached out his hand with two small items in it and said, "Here. You have clearance. Use the employee entrance from now on. Follow me." Steve and Jim said nothing as they got back on the elevator and went down to John's office floor and into the lab. He pulled out the evidence bag, opened it, and placed it on a white screen. The document was projected onto a white board in front of them, and Jim and Steve's jaws dropped when they saw what was on it.

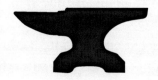

CHAPTER THREE

*"We have a killer, gentlemen,
and that killer has just declared
war on the LAPD."*

Marco had moved out of the store and was standing next to his cruiser with Andre. They were speaking quietly, however, in the public eye. "What the fuck, man?" Andre said with a bitter tone in his voice. "What the fuck?...I'll tell you what the fuck... You call me before you make any moves, any decisions, and you sure as hell call me when you got word on the street about Alverez's replacement." "Not here!" "Get in my fuckin' car." Andre pulled the passenger door open and got in. Marco sat down in the driver's seat and asked, "Well?" "Well...what the fuck, Marco? I've been under deep cover for almost a year, and you're going to come in and blow everything out of the water? Do you know the wrath of shit you will bring down on us with Captain Boyd? Jesus Christ! We are sitting in a fucking parking lot in the middle of East LA. Do you really think this is the place to have this conversation?"

Marco looked around at the faces staring at the two of them in the cruiser. "Um…yea. What the hell? Tell me what I want to know!" "Jesus Christ, Marco, you just signed my death warrant." "All the more reason to tell me what you know." "I don't have a name. Several members of Alberto's family are coming up from Mexico, now that the funeral is done, to make a decision." Marco handed Andre a piece of paper and said, "Names…write down the names and then get the fuck out of my car." Andre wrote quickly in Spanish and went to get out of the cruiser. "WAIT!" Marco said, "you forgot something." Andre took the paper and wrote several more things. Marco took the paper and looked it over and said, "Good, very good. I want the family names, but I also need the names of the mules that are bringing the drugs. Good boy. Now, get out of the car." Andre said, "Fuck you, asshole. I'm going to kick your ass the next time I see you at the station."

Andre got out, as did Marco. He walked around the front of the car and said, "Don't worry. I'm about to save your life." He started yelling at Andre in Spanish for everyone to hear. He watched as people began to congregate on the streets and porches of homes, and he pulled out his police baton and began to beat Andre with it, all the while yelling at him. The growing crowd started to get angry as Marco yelled insults at Andre and beat him. He kicked Andre in the ribs and pulled him close to his face and whispered, "You will be sore tomorrow, but you will be alive." Andre winced as he was pushed against the pavement. He whispered back, "Payback is a bitch, Marco." With that, Marco put the baton back in his car and drove away.

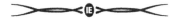

"The PIGS of the Los Angeles Police Department have lived long enough!" was the headline of the document retrieved from the coat jacket of LAPD Detective Mario Sanchez. The pamphlet found in his pocket was a typed and printed list of LA cops and internal affairs officers. John said, "We have a killer, gentlemen, and that killer has just declared war on

the LAPD." Jim laughed, taking a cigarette out of his top left pocket and said, "This might be the killer's formal declaration of war, but whoever this is has fired the first shot!" Steve was looking at the note and reading the names. John saw that Steve was intense, and he asked, "What do you see, Steve?" John looked back at the screen and the list of names. Steve started to recite the names of the killer's targets.

"Mary Schultz, Internal Affairs LAPD (deceased); Mario Sanchez, Detective LAPD (now deceased); Gilbert Chavez, Detective LAPD; Howard Washington, Patrol Officer LAPD; Patricia Salazar, Detective and Internal Affairs Officer LAPD; Brian Boyd, Captain LAPD, Internal Affairs and police union president; Harry Chilton, Lieutenant LAPD Homicide Supervisor and Field Investigator; Ricardo Pina, Public Relations Officer LAPD; Vince Espeno, Deputy Chief of Police LAPD; Albert Ralston, Chief of Police LAPD."

"Jesus Christ, men! This killer is going to take out the central command of the LAPD." Steve said it with an air of both frustration and anger. John looked on at the names listed on the screen as Jim chomped on the smoke between his teeth.

John sat down, staring at the screen, and said, "Okay, so we have a hit list. The question is how do we keep the rest of these folks alive while hunting this killer?" Jim let out a little laugh, and John shot him a look, "What's so funny?" Jim leaned back in his chair and said, "I know, or in the case of the first two, knew, these people, and I can tell you they were dirty cops." Steve looked at him and asked, "Now just how the fuck do you know that?" Jim laughed, "John and I were recently appointed as county and federal independent consultants to a case of a cop that the people on this list were targeting." Steve looked at the list and said, "What happened?" "They fired him!" Steve smiled and said, "Well, there you go. You know the killer's name?" Jim nodded and said, "Well, fuck, the case is solved. Send someone out to pick him up." He laughed, and John interrupted, "We can't, Jim, and you know that." Steve got a pissed off look on his face and asked, "Why the fuck not?" "Because he's already in jail," Jim said

with a smart-ass tone in his voice. "Who's in jail?" Steve asked. "The victim of those named on that list. His name is Garrison Cantrell. He's been in jail since we found the body of Mary Schultz. LAPD hung her murder around his neck like a medallion," Jim said, taking the smoke out of his mouth and putting it behind his ear.

Steve looked thoughtfully and asked, "Where's Garrison now?" "Men's central jail, but his attorney has filed a motion to have him taken into federal custody until he can be tried as he is pleading not guilty, and there is fear for his safety," Jim said as he stood up to stretch his legs. "Who's the judge?" Steve asked. "Tracy Olson," John replied, "I'm going to be at the hearing to argue that he needs to be in protective custody until his case can be heard." Steve nodded slowly and said, "The cops will kill him. I'm surprised he's still alive." Jim laughed and said, "My deputies are watching over him; however, given this new twist in the case, I think Mr. Cantrell is not the one who has an axe to grind. I think we need to take a long look at the evidence in the two killings. I think LAPD is trying to railroad an innocent man." John started laughing as he looked at his watch. "What did you do with Jim O'Brian? Where did he go? Are you some kind of pod person? Jim never thinks anyone is innocent." Steve laughed and coughed a little, as did Jim who looked at John and said, "Go fuck yourself, asshole!"

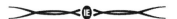

John and Steve arrived at the LA Superior Court for Cantrell's hearing at eight thirty a.m. They were waved past security, and John was able to push Steve into an elevator that took them to the third floor and Judge Tracy Olson's courtroom. He pushed Steve to the front and said, "I will be right back. I want to see if I can speak to the judge before anyone else gets in." Steve nodded and sat in his wheelchair staring at the seal of the State of California behind the judge's bench.

John walked over to the judge's clerk, who frowned when he saw him approach. "Special Agent Swenson, to what do we owe the honor of your presence?" "Good morning, Bill. I wanted to have a few

moments with Tracy before she takes the bench in the Cantrell case."
Bill Gibbons had been Judge Olson's clerk since she was appointed to
fill a vacancy on the bench after the death of Marion Davis in the Los
Angeles fires nearly three years earlier. John and Tracy had a history.
They dated for about six months many years ago. Tracy wanted more,
and John could not commit. He was an LAPD officer then, and since
the breakup, and then John's marriage to Sara, which went over like a
lead balloon, tensions between Tracy and John ran high.

Through all of it, though, John and Tracy managed to keep a
professional relationship. Bill buzzed her chambers and announced
Agent Swenson. There was a moment of silence and an attorney
approached Bill's desk and was standing right on John's heels. He
turned to see that it was Howard Cohen, whom he greeted with a smile
and a handshake before Bill told John, "The judge will see you now."
John waved goodbye to Howard and walked off to the sheriff-guarded
door and onto the judge's chambers. Howard looked at Bill and said,
"WOW! I bet that's going to be an awkward meeting." Bill looked on,
taking Howard's business card, and said, "Ya think?"

John rapped on Tracy's door, and she called out, "Come in, Agent
Swenson." John opened the door and walked into the dimly lit room. The
blinds were closed, and Judge Olson was sitting at her desk with a cloth
over her eyes and a cup of coffee in her hands. "Migraine?" John asked.
"Oh yes, John, a major mother fuckin' migraine." "Why didn't you call
in?" "John, we have hardly any judges on the bench. There is no way I
can call in sick with the backlog of cases we are handling. Now, please,
I beg you, get to the point of why you're in my chambers." She took a
sip of the coffee and as she did, John reached into his pocket and pulled
out a small pillbox. Olson shuddered at the noise, but John opened it and
took out a large blue capsule, walked over, and handed it to her. "What's
this?" "Just take it…it's fast acting, and the migraine will be gone." She
didn't ask any questions. She popped the pill in her mouth and took two
big sips of her coffee. She went to say something and John said, "Five
minutes, Tracy. Give it five minutes, and then we can talk."

John sat down on one of the leather chairs in front of her desk and admired her legs that were up on a stool. She was a very beautiful woman. Her long red hair was down below her shoulders, and her green eyes set off well against her tanning bed tan and her pursed lips. She was in a light blue blouse and a matching short skirt. He watched and waited until she pulled her legs off the stool and sat up and asked, "What the hell did you give me?" "Nothing you haven't taken before for your head." He stood up and opened the blinds to the three windows in her corner chambers and let the morning sunlight flood in.

She was bright-eyed and smiling. Tracy got up and walked over and gave him a hug and a kiss on the cheek and said, "Thank you... you are a godsend today." He smiled and sat back down and said, "Your honor, I'm here on the Cantrell case." She sat back down in her chair and said, "Cut the formalities, John. I know why you're here, and I'm going to grant the motion to have the suspect remanded into federal hands this morning." "Thank you, Tracy. I will take him over to the federal building after the hearing, if that's okay with you?" "Yea. No problem. So, how are you and Sara doing?"

John smiled and said, "We are doing well. Sara is putting in a lot of hours, but she is doing really, really well." "You haven't been a slouch yourself. That was a hell of a case that you and Jim broke up out in Devil's Chair." He nodded. "I have to admit I've been puking my guts out now and again every time I think of the meats I ate and the cheeses I purchased that they produced. I haven't had the opportunity to thank you for that. I'm nearly at my goal weight!" They both laughed, and she said, "Now, get out of my chambers. I have to be on the bench in five minutes." He stood up, and Tracy looked at him and said, "God, I miss you." John got a sad look on his face and said, "If I had been ready to settle down back then, Tracy, I would have settled down with you. But I wasn't, and by the time I was, you were in a relationship, and I found Sara again. I did love you and still do. If you ever need anything, all you have to do is call me." She nodded as John walked out of her office.

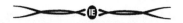

"All rise. This court will come to order. The Honorable Judge Tracy Olson presiding." Tracy walked in in her black robe and sat down in the judge's chair. "Clerk, please call the first case!" "The people versus Garrison Cantrell." Tracy looked over to see Cantrell in jailhouse clothing sitting next to his counsel. The prosecutor, Mary Rogers, was standing at attention in a sharp suit. She shot John a dirty look as the court was ordered seated.

Benson Santone was seated next to Garrison. Tracy spoke, "I have read the briefs supplied to me by both sides. While I know that Ms. Rogers would like to have Mr. Cantrell remain in the custody of the sheriff's department, I have to side with Mr. Santone that Mr. Cantrell's life could be in jeopardy given the volatile situation that this case brings, and, therefore, I am ordering him to be remanded over to the federal authorities for holding pending trial."

Much to John and Steve's surprise, as well as many others in the courtroom, there was no objection. The judge was just about to slam the gavel when Santone rose to address the court. "Your honor, in light of recent events, I am making a motion for dismissal of all charges against my client." The bailiff walked over and took a document from Santone's hand and brought it to the judge. John looked over at Rogers, who sat silent. Santone handed a copy of the motion to Rogers, who sat and read it. Judge Olson read the motion and then asked, "Ms. Rogers, have you had an opportunity to see this motion?" "I have, your honor. The people acknowledge that the killing of Detective Sanchez and Officer Schultz were acknowledged in a note left for law enforcement after the cold-blooded murder of Detective Sanchez."

Santone spoke, "Your honor, there is not one piece of solid evidence against Mr. Cantrell. The State's case has been based on circumstantial evidence, which, based on the tragic murder of Detective Sanchez, proves that my client had nothing to do with Ms. Schultz's death. Mr. Cantrell has had his Fifth Amendment rights trampled by the court and

the police in this matter. He has committed no crime. The State has a new suspect that must be sought out. The record is clear, your honor, and that record shows that Mr. Cantrell could not have committed Schultz's murder or the murder of Detective Sanchez. We hereby move for dismissal of all charges against my client with prejudice."

Rogers sounded off with a volley of her own, and when the smoke cleared, John could see that Olson did have a bit of a pickle on her hands. "Mr. Santone, while I understand your argument, the State has filed serious charges against Mr. Cantrell." "Charges that are trumped up and without basis or support in law, your honor. My client should not have to sit in prison awaiting trial for a crime he clearly did not commit." Olson pulled a penal code book from behind her desk and opened it and pored over it, looking up the cases cited by Santone in his motion.

Rogers started to interrupt her, and Olson shot her down. "Mr. Santone cites proper points and authorities that do make it difficult, if not illegal, to hold Mr. Cantrell in jail. While I will not dismiss the case against Mr. Cantrell, I do believe that significant modification of his custody is in order. I am ordering Mr. Cantrell released on his own recognizance with the agreement that he will wear a digital ankle tracker. Mr. Cantrell will be free to move about at his whim. He has already surrendered his passport, and as Mr. Santone points out in his motion, Mr. Cantrell does not pose a flight risk. I also feel that recent events give this court pause in this matter, and that keeping Mr. Cantrell in custody would be a violation of his constitutional rights. Therefore, it is the order of this court that the terms of Mr. Cantrell's bail be amended as stated. He shall be remanded to pretrial release and be fitted with a GPS tracking ankle bracelet and monitored by the California Department of Probation."

Rogers argued momentarily, but she knew it was getting her nowhere. Judge Olson said, "Mr. Cantrell, please rise." He did as instructed. "Do you understand the modified terms of your release?" "Yes, your honor." "Do you understand that if you do not immediately upon release present yourself to the department of probation you will have violated the terms of your pretrial release, and you will

be reincarcerated?" "Yes, your honor." "You may be seated." Olson rattled off the modifications for the record, slammed her gavel down, and told the court it would be in recess for ten minutes. She stood up and walked off the bench and back to her chambers.

Steve looked at John and asked, "What the fuck did you say to her?" John shrugged. "Nothing. She had a migraine headache, and I gave her a little something to get rid of the headache." Steve looked at John and said, "You drugged her?" "Well…not exactly. The medicine would not have affected her judgment. I did forget that about an hour after taking that medication most people end up throwing up." "You mean she's puking in the toilet?" John stood up and waited for Cantrell and said to Steve, "It's unlikely that she made it to the bathroom. I would say that someone is calling for cleanup on hallway three." Steve started laughing as John pulled his ID and asked to speak to Mr. Santone and Mr. Cantrell.

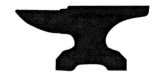

CHAPTER FOUR

*"Then the question isn't who wanted to
kill him…it's more like who didn't."*

It was ten after nine, and Detective Gilbert Chavez walked out of
Union Station in downtown LA. He liked to take the train. It was
convenient and within walking distance of his office near the federal
courthouse on Spring Street. He had been assigned to an annex office
after the fires in the San Fernando Valley destroyed his office. He was
really enjoying the new office. It was close to Olvera Street off Spring
Street where he stopped every morning for a Mexican breakfast.

The Tortilla Shack had been on Olvera Street for generations,
serving breakfast, lunch, and dinner right near the end of the tourist
section of the street. Gil walked up to the window to order, and a
man in a chef's uniform with a white hat and sunglasses greeted him.
"Where's Mario?" Gil asked inquisitively. "He's ill today, and he
asked me to fill in for him." "How can I get my usual when Mario
is not here to make it?" The chef had a piece of paper in front of
him on the counter and said, "He left me this list of his regulars

with instructions on their meals. What's your name, sir?" "Chavez." "Detective Gilbert Chavez?" He nodded. "It will be but a moment, sir. One special Mexican burrito coming right up."

Chavez walked over to one of the benches and sat down. The sun was rising, and it always shined right into the window of the shop. Gil said to himself, "Mario is probably home with a migraine from years in the sun." He grabbed a discarded morning paper and was reading over the headlines when he read that Mario Sanchez had been killed. He read the article, holding the paper with both hands and shaking. He put the paper down and said, "Shit...first Schultz, now Mario. Who's next?" He had just finished verbalizing the thought when he heard his name called. He walked up to the pickup window and took the bag from the chef. He started to walk off when the man called out and asked, "Aren't you forgetting something?" Gilbert looked back and said, "Oh, shit. I totally forgot. You're right. Where's my large black coffee?" "No, detective," the man said while pouring the large coffee and placing a lid on it, "you forgot to pay." Chavez started laughing and said, "Mario never charges me. I'm a police officer. I protect this little slice of heaven for him and the others." "Protect?" The chef's face was expressionless. "Yea," Chavez said while unwrapping the burrito and taking a bite. The chef leaned down and put his thin arms on the counter and asked, "Protection from what?"

Chavez had a mouth full of food and egg was spilling out as he spoke, "That's for me and Mario and the others to know, and for you to mind your own damn business." There were a few moments of silence, and Gilbert bit into something hard in his burrito. "Ouch..." He pulled the object from the stuffing and showed it to the chef. "Sorry. A bit of underdone green bell pepper. Do you want me to make you another?" Chavez waved him off and said, "I don't have time, asshole. Learn to cook. I will speak to Mario about it tomorrow when I see him." He walked off sipping his coffee and swallowing the bites that were too tough for his teeth. He walked across the street to his office and was about to enter the building when he got a sudden stomach cramp. He leaned against the wall for a few seconds, and it passed. He got his composure and went inside.

Steve and John took Garrison to one of the conference rooms off the courtroom and asked him to sit. Santone followed, and neither John nor Steve said a word. They sat down, and before John could speak, Garrison said, "I never got the opportunity to thank you and Sheriff O'Brian for defending me in the internal affairs investigation and eventual railroading of my career." "I'm sorry about that, Mr. Cantrell. I wish there was more that I could have done." Cantrell laughed. "There was nothing that anyone could do. That decision was made months in advance of that meeting."

Steve spoke up and said, "That's what we want to talk to you about." Garrison smiled and folded his hands on the table and said, "So…talk." "Ms. Schultz is not the only person on that panel who is dead. Now we have the body of Detective Sanchez." Garrison looked and said, "I heard about it. His head was blown clean off." John nodded and asked, "Do you know of anyone who would have wanted to kill him?" Garrison started laughing in hysterics. It took several minutes to get his composure back, and he said, "You're kidding, right? Is this some kind of joke? Were you two on his crime scene?" They nodded. "Then the question isn't who wanted to kill him…it's more like who didn't. I have known Sanchez a long time. He was a brutal and sadistic man. Cruel doesn't begin to describe him." John asked, "Do you have any theories on who might have killed him?" Garrison smirked and said, "Well, we know it wasn't me."

The smile left his face as he continued, "Sanchez is dead because of his own bravado. He ran a dangerous game with some dangerous people. A person in a position of authority can't run the kind of schemes he was running – they are running – and expect that there won't be consequences. Detective Sanchez is dead because he had no honor. He had no compassion, and he had no concern for human dignity. Do I have any idea who killed him? No. The list of people who would want him dead is wide and varied."

Steve asked, "And Schultz?" Santone sat up in his chair, but he didn't say anything. Garrison looked at the two men and said, "It's the same thing. She was watching her pockets and not her back, but God was watching, and she got what was coming to her." "Enough," Santone said. Garrison looked on and said, "What, Ben? I didn't kill the woman. I have an alibi. They might as well know the truth." Santone admonished Garrison again, but he just shook his head. "Look, gentlemen, I know that you came here today to take me into federal custody to protect me. I'm blown away that the judge has allowed me to be released, but it won't change what's happening."

John leaned forward and said, "What's happening?" Garrison said, "The sins of the many have been or are being discovered. If you ask me who is doing the killing…it's the Iron Eagle." John sat back in his chair and looked Garrison in the eye and said, "I know the Iron Eagle very, very well…at least his profile, and I can tell you this is not the work of the Eagle."

Garrison shrugged and said, "You asked who I thought was doing the killing, and I told you. None of it matters because I'm next. I might be out of jail, but they are going to kill me because they think that will keep their secrets safe." "What secret?" John asked. "Secrets. Plural, Agent Swenson. It won't work. Someone else knows of their sins, and a lot more are going to die, and there's nothing you, the FBI, or the sheriff's department can do to stop it."

Steve rolled away from the table and said, "It's our job to seek out and capture these types of killers. We will find him and capture him and bring him to justice." Garrison just smiled and said, "I hope so, but I highly doubt it. I assume by now he has left you a list."

John asked, "A list?" "Yes, a list. A list of his intended victims. He will kill them in order, so if you want to stop the carnage before it really gets going, you might want to put surveillance on the living targets. Who knows? You might just get lucky." Garrison stood up and said, "If you will excuse me, I need to get to the probation department, so I comply with the terms of my pretrial release." Garrison walked out with Santone behind him.

John and Steve sat alone in the outer room, and Steve said, "Something isn't right with that guy." John nodded, saying, "You picked up on that, too!" John stood up and got behind Steve and pushed his wheelchair out of the room and to a waiting elevator. "He's right, John. We need to get surveillance on the living people on the list." "It's not our jurisdiction." The elevator was empty and quiet as the two rode down to the ground floor and headed out to John's truck. After John got Steve situated, he started driving back to Westwood and the federal building. Steve said, "When has jurisdiction ever stopped the Iron fuckin' Eagle? This is his jurisdiction." John nodded as they drove back to the office.

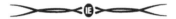

Jade Morgan was dictating the last of her autopsy notes on the Sanchez murder when Andre Espinoza called back to her office from the front lobby of the new Los Angeles County Coroner's office. She got up and walked out to see Andre leaning on the counter. "Andre, what are you doing here? I thought you were under deep cover?" she said with a little bit of attitude. "Hey, can't an old friend just stop in and see how another old friend is doing?" She leaned on the counter across from him and said, "Yea...come on back. I don't have time to fool around though."

He followed her into her office where she took off her lab coat and sat down in her chair. She was wearing a very seductive purple top, showing ample cleavage, and he sat staring. "My eyes are up here, Andre. What do you want?" He shook his head and laughed. "Sorry, but you put those babies on parade, and you expect a guy to look at your face? I mean you are stunningly beautiful, but, Jade, my God...I look at your chest and all I can think of is whack-a-doodle!" She started laughing and said, "Do you want me to put my lab coat back on?" "No...no...good God NO!" "WHAT...DO...YOU...WANT?" Jade asked again. "You got Sanchez's body yesterday, right?" She nodded. "Did you find anything?" Jade sat back in her chair and looked at Andre

with a baffled look on her face. "Andre…you're a fuckin' detective and an undercover one at that. You're a hot looking hunk of a Latin man and a hell of a lover, but this is not even in your ballpark."

He smiled, his white teeth like a light against his skin and deep brown eyes. "Hey…I knew him. He was a friend, and, besides, I saw him just before he got whacked yesterday." Jade sat up. "When did you see him?" "I was over in Koreatown rousting some of the kids from the East side. They were planning a drive by, and I found out about it. I parked my car out of sight and was walking across the street from the market and saw him pull in and go inside." "Fuck! Have you told anyone about this?" "Hey, I said I knew the guy. I didn't say I liked him. He was a dirty cop. If you ask me, he got what was coming to him, and it was a long time coming."

Jade stood, and she was pissed. "I didn't ask you that. I asked if you told anyone that you saw Detective Sanchez go into the market." The smile left his face, and he sat up straight. His powerful shoulders bulged in his uniform. "No…I didn't tell anyone. Are you happy?" "Were you there when he was shot?" There was a hesitation, and then he said, "No…no…I found the kids and got them off the street and back to the East side." "Where were you when Sanchez was shot?" Jade asked. "Jesus Christ! Are you a fuckin' cop now, Jade? Just because you live with an FBI agent doesn't make you a fuckin' cop…or does it?"

Jade looked angry and indignant and said, "I don't live with an FBI agent. I live in one of the guesthouses. He and his wife happen to be close friends of mine. I'm not a cop, but when a man I sleep with as a casual friend tells me he was on a murder scene before the murder, I want to know why he hasn't told anyone."

Andre stood and straightened his uniform. "You want to know why I didn't tell anyone? Because no one gives a shit. He was dirty. Everyone in West Valley knew it. I'm not going to rat out that I saw him and then get pegged for his killing like Garrison Cantrell did. Fuck that shit." He walked over to the side of her desk and leaned down next to her and whispered, "You better not tell anyone what I told you either. There's a lot of shit going down right now, and you could become a casualty of this situation."

He stood up and started for the door. Jade stood and said, "Did you just threaten me? Did you just mother fuckin' threaten me, Andre?" He kept walking as he talked, "I'm just speaking the mother fuckin' truth, babe. I'm just speaking the truth." He laughed under his breath but loud enough for Jade to hear. As soon as his cruiser was out of the parking lot, she called John.

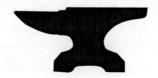

CHAPTER FIVE

"You're never going to believe this.
It's fuckin' Chavez. He collapsed
while taking a shit."

Gil Chavez was doubled over in pain while in the bathroom sitting on the toilet. It had been an hour since he ate breakfast, and he was cursing Mario and his helper, whoever the guy was, for the bad burrito. A couple of other officers were in the bathroom with him and all were cracking jokes about eating on Olvera Street. "You know, Gil, you might want to give up on the spicy food for a while!" a voice said from the other side of the stall. "Oh, fuck you, Martin. You're an asshole. I'm shitting razor blades in here." Gil stood, and he felt his legs go out from underneath him. He passed out and hit the floor sliding down the front of the stall until his head and upper body were outside the door. There was laughter, which turned to calls for help as blood started to pool around Chavez's head and body. "Holy fuckin' shit…call 911. Call 911."

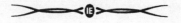

Jim was sitting on the smoker's bench having a cigarette in front of his office when his cell phone rang. "O'Brian." He listened for a few seconds and then started laughing. "You're shittin' me; you're fuckin' shittin' me. They want me at the West Valley division temporary offices at the federal building of LAPD?" There were a few more moments of silence, and he said, "I'm on my way. This I gotta see." He hung up the phone and called out to one of his detectives. "I'm on my way over to the federal court building. Let everyone know I will call it in when I get there." Jim was laughing with the cigarette still in his mouth as he started the car and headed further downtown. He was mumbling, "This I just have to see. This will be one for the record books."

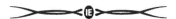

John and Steve had just gotten back to the office when John's cell rang. "Swenson." "John, it's Jade." "Hey, Jade. What's going on?" He could tell she was out of breath as if she was scared. "Are you okay? What's going on?" She caught her breath and said, "Listen, you know that cop I've been dating out of West Valley?" "I don't know him. I've seen his cruiser at the house a few times. Why?" "His name is Andre Espinoza. He was just in here asking questions about the Sanchez murder."

John was quiet for a second then asked, "He's a detective, right?" "Yes…he came in to see me. I thought he wanted a nooner, but he really wanted to ask about Sanchez." "What about him?" "It never got that far. He told me that he was in Koreatown yesterday, and that he saw Sanchez go into the market." "That's the first I'm hearing of a cop seeing Sanchez yesterday before he was killed." "Yea, well, it gets stranger. When I started to probe him and asked him if he told anyone he was there and saw Sanchez, he told me no, and then he threatened me."

John was silent for a second and asked, "How did he threaten you?" "He said I better keep my mouth shut about him seeing Sanchez. He said there is a lot of weird shit going on, and I could end up in the middle of it." "Interesting…where does Sanchez usually work out of?"

"He works East LA. He handles a lot of the gang shit now that it's reemerging in LA. Turf wars and shit like that." "Did he say why he was in Koreatown?" Jade explained it all to him and when she was finished she said, "John, I'm scared." "Relax. You have a staff. Don't go to your car alone, and when you're home on property keep your alarm set on the house. I will have security step up patrols on the house inside and out if that's okay with you?" "Absolutely, John. I have known Andre for a few years, and the man that was talking to me in my office was not the Andre that I know." "Okay. I got the information you gave me. I will run it down and see what I can find on him and his whereabouts yesterday." Jade thanked him and hung up the line.

John hung up and called Jim's cell. "O'Brian." "Hey, Jim, where are you?" "You will never believe where I am. I am walking into the federal building where West Valley has a temporary station because one of their cops was just life-flighted to the only trauma center in LA." "An officer is down in LA, and they are flying him to Northridge?" "You got it. I was told that Sara and Karen had been called in to meet the chopper. I don't know much else. You want to come down and slum with me here?" "Do you know who it is and what happened?" "Hang on. The paramedics are still on scene as well as officers."

John heard the phone go quiet as if Jim was covering the mouthpiece. Then Jim must have pulled it away from his body, and John could hear him yelling, "Hey, who the fuck did I get called down here for? Is this a goddamn homicide, or is someone busting my fuckin' balls?" Jim came back a few seconds later and said, "You're never going to believe this. It's fuckin' Chavez. He collapsed while taking a shit. They said there was blood everywhere. You coming down?" "No...I'm heading for Northridge Hospital. I need to talk to Chavez if I can. Call me once you know more. I will call you when I know something."

He hung up the phone and ran out the door with his suit coat over his arm. "Tell Steve I will be back, and that I had to run out for a few minutes." He disappeared into an open elevator. Steve was wheeling himself down the hall when he saw John heading out. He stopped at the field agent's desk

and asked, "What the hell was that all about?" She shrugged her shoulders and said, "If I didn't know John better, I would think he was going to get laid!" Steve laughed and wheeled himself back to his office.

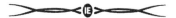

Sara and Karen were standing on the helipad at Northridge Hospital as the chopper touched down. They followed Gilbert Chavez's gurney into the ER. They were both checking him and barking out instructions. Karen yelled, "Get me five units of O negative, stat. Do a type and cross on this patient, stat as well." The ER was humming, and within a few minutes they had Chavez, nude, on a gurney. He was bleeding out his rectum and his mouth. He was barely conscious. Sara was calling to him through the oxygen mask over his face. "Mr. Chavez, what happened?" He choked out the word, "burrito" as he struggled to breathe. Karen asked, "Did you eat a burrito?" He nodded slowly as he was losing consciousness. Sara yelled out, "We need to get him to an operating room, stat." Karen was running alongside Sara as they rushed Gilbert into the OR. The doors closed behind them as they tried to intubate him, but they could not get a clear airway. "There's too much blood. His throat has been cut from the inside." One of the other doctors said, "Let's trach him." Sara called out to Karen. Chavez was going fast, and there was no way to keep him breathing or to find the source of the bleed. He died on the table, and Karen called out the TOD.

The two looked at each other and walked out of the operating room to see John standing in the hall. "How is he?" "Dead," Sara said. "What killed him?" Karen shook her head and said, "We will have to wait for autopsy to know. He bled out. That's all I can tell you. He just bled out."

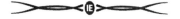

Jade had just gotten her lunch and was preparing to eat it when she was paged that she had a call. She picked up a phone in the lounge and said, "Morgan." "Jade, I need you at Northridge Hospital right

away." John's voice was calm, cool, and collected, and that unnerved Jade. "What's going on?" "I need an autopsy on a dead police officer, and I need it now." Jade took a bite of her salad and asked, "If he died in a hospital, why me? Just have one of the doctors do the autopsy. Northridge is a California certified crime lab." "I want you. I need you here, Jade, and I need you here now." She put the lid on her salad while holding the phone to her ear. "Okay, John, okay…I'm on my way. Who's the attending?" "Sara and Karen." "Jesus, John. Karen was in on this? What happened?" "They don't know. I don't know. I have Jim on scene at the office where the officer collapsed, and all that Sara and Karen could tell me is that he bled out." Jade opened the refrigerator to put the salad away and asked, "Is it anyone I know?" "I don't think so. The guy's name is Gilbert Chavez." There was no immediate response. "Jade, are you still on the line?" "Um…yea…yea…I'm on my way." She hung up the phone with tears in her eyes and headed out the door to her coroner's car and Northridge Hospital.

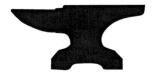

CHAPTER SIX

"The notion of innocent until proven
guilty is just that, isn't it Ben?"

arrison Cantrell arrived at the federal probation department with
his attorney in tow. Probation Officer Don Bartell was expecting
Cantrell and invited him back to his office. "Okay…Mr. Cantrell,
while you are on informal monitoring, it is still monitoring." Bartell took
a small black box with a strap on it and handed it to Garrison. "This is a
GPS transmitter. It is satellite-activated. Once it is attached to you, it will
transmit your whereabouts at all times to me and all other monitoring
offices. While you have no travel restrictions in the state of California,
the unit will notify me and others if you venture out of LA County."

Bartell had a tablet in front of him, and he took the unit back from
Cantrell, ran a scanner over a barcode reader on the unit, and there was
a beep. Bartell got up and walked over to Cantrell and asked which leg
he wanted the unit on. He pointed to his left leg. Bartell leaned down
and snapped the unit in place, leaving Garrison a little wiggle room to
move the unit up or down. "Okay, so, you are live." Bartell looked at

his computer tablet and showed it to Garrison. "You see this blinking red dot?" Cantrell nodded. "That's you. From here on out, until your trial, or if you are otherwise released from the program, I can see your every move. Do you have any business planned out of state?" Cantrell shook his head. "Do you have any business that will take you out of Los Angeles, Orange, Riverside, Ventura, San Bernardino, or San Diego Counties?" Cantrell shook his head again. "Okay, well then, you are good to go. Here is a pamphlet on your device. It's waterproof, so you can bathe and swim if you like. There is nothing that you need to do to check in, though you should have your cell phone with you at all times in the event that I call. Um…you will see me once a month until your trial. I will send you an email for your calendar. Do you have any questions?" "Yea… what if I get tired of having this on, and I cut it off?" "Oh, that's an easy one – you go to jail until your trial. Tampering with the unit in any way, shape, or form will be an immediate violation of your release, and you will go directly to jail. Does that answer your question?" "Um…yea, pretty much." "Good. You are dismissed." Bartell stood up and opened his office door to show Cantrell out. As they left the office, Garrison said, "The notion of innocent until proven guilty is just that, isn't it Ben?" "Oh, yes, Garrison, oh yes. It truly is." Garrison Cantrell just shook his head as the two men left the probation office.

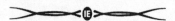

Lance Coswalski was revving up the engine on one of the Harley Davidsons that he rented out to tourists near Balboa Park in the San Fernando Valley. He had kept a low profile since working with John and the others in operations Rome is Burning and Red Alert. He liked the nice private life he was enjoying in the private sector. He had plenty of money, so he could do what he loved. He had just turned off the bike when an all too familiar grating voice yelled out to him. "So, are we going to rent the son of a bitch out, or are you going to buy it a dress and take it out for dinner?"

Lance looked up to see his friend and business partner, Patrick Martin, leaning against the doorway to the garage where he was working on the bike. Lance looked at him and asked, "Why didn't I kill you when I had the chance?" "Because you're a pussy and too slow on the draw. Now, I have a customer who wants the damn bike. Is it ready?" Lance pushed the bike into the show room where the customer was waiting.

Howard Washington was in his police uniform with his motorcycle helmet under his arm. Lance parked the bike, and Patrick asked Washington, "So, you're a bike cop. Why are you renting this baby when you ride the same bike all day?" Washington was running his hand along the fuel tank and said, "Because I ride one all day and because my police issue bike is not like the street bike. I want to make sure that it's what I want before I make the investment."

Lance laughed and said, "Buying a bike is like getting married; you better know what you're getting into because if it goes bad, you never get out of them what you put into them." Patrick rolled his eyes, and Washington laughed under his breath and said, "Ain't that the truth."

Washington was an impressive figure at six eight and three hundred pounds. He was also the quintessential motorcycle cop. His bald head and imposing figure had been known to scare more than motorists. He got on the bike and asked, "Is it okay if I take it for a spin?" Patrick said sure and opened the double doors. Washington took off down Reseda Boulevard at full speed, and Lance said, "It would be nice to have that kind of immunity to the law."

Patrick just laughed and said, "He has immunity to the law because we allowed him to keep his freedom." Lance nodded and walked back into the garage to work on another bike. Washington was back in five minutes and paid for one month's rent and took off south on Reseda headed to Ventura Boulevard.

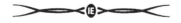

Marco Estrada was standing at the corner of Reseda and Ventura when he saw Washington sitting at the light. He had his cruiser parked off on Reseda, and he ran across traffic and hit Howard on the back. Howard jumped and went for his weapon when he turned to see Estrada standing next to him in full uniform. Howard put his hands up in a 'what the fuck' gesture, and Estrada pointed to the parking lot of Tarzana market across the street. Howard nodded, and Estrada ran back to his cruiser then turned on his lights to cross traffic and led Howard to the lot. Once they parked, Howard got off the bike and started yelling at Estrada. "What the fuck, man? Shit. I nearly shot your Mexican ass!" "Oh, fuck you, you big ass nigger. I saw you and wanted to stop you before you got killed crossing the intersection."

Washington looked and asked, "What the fuck are you talking about?" "Your left turn signal is out, dumb ass, and if you had tried to make a turn, oncoming traffic would not know your ass was turning, and you would be yet another cop biker death." Washington checked out the blinker and saw that it wasn't working, and he looked at Estrada and said, "Thanks, man. You're not too bad for a spic!" "Yea, well, you know how it is. If us spics don't look out for you spear chuckers, who would?" They shared a laugh, and Howard asked, "What the fuck, man? What the hell are you doing in Sherman Oaks?" "I'm off duty and was going to the bank and saw your sorry ass about to get killed. I live south of the boulevard past Ventura." Howard looked at him and said, "When did you move into this high class suburb?" "Shit, man… my wife and I bought a lot after the fires and had a house built. We have some great views. You should come up and see it some time." "No fucking way, man…I figure whitey would have a heart attack if he saw a nigger and a spic at the same house in white bread land."

They laughed, and Estrada said, "Yea…when we first started building, those homes that had survived the fire were all whites. When they saw me and the wife and kids pull up, I heard one of them say, 'There goes the neighborhood.' The next day, I pulled up in my police cruiser to check out the lot before construction, and suddenly whitey

was all kinds of happy. They had a cop in the neighborhood." Howard laughed and said, "So, did you put some fuzzy dice in your car, so they'd know you were Mexican?" "Oh hell yea, man…I got it all cholloed out! What's up with the street bike?" "I'm thinking about buying one, but I want to see how the street bike rides as opposed to my police bike." "And?" "And…I have had it for all of…" he looked at his watch, "ten minutes, so I can't say for sure. I'm off duty. I have some business to attend to, and then I will take it up to my house in Northridge."

Estrada laughed and said, "I didn't know they were letting niggers into my old turf." "Oh yea, the brothers are taking over the spic's turf. It's only a matter of time before we have a hip-hop and rap studio going and some brothers with their bling walking the streets of the hood."

Estrada laughed and said, "Well, unlike you worthless dogs, I have to work. Ride safe." He patted Howard on the shoulder and slipped a flyer in his leather jacket pocket. Howard saw him do it and asked, "What the fuck, man?" "It's a fundraiser the West Valley Department is putting on. I thought you could show up there with your police bike and WOW the little kids." Howard just laughed and rode off. Estrada stood there smiling, watching as Howard pulled out of the lot onto Reseda headed for Northridge.

Jade walked out of the hospital morgue with a small white towel. John was waiting for her. She was still in surgical scrubs and covered in blood. "So?" John asked. Jade handed him the towel, and he opened it slowly. There, in the towel, were three small green balls. He recognized them right away. "Sulfuric acid tablets…Jesus I haven't seen these in a few years." Jade looked at John with a strange look on her face and asked, "You know what this is?" He nodded. "How could you know?" she asked. "It was part of my training in the Marine Corps and with the FBI." "What…were they training you to use it to kill people?" John looked on and asked, "So, this is what killed Chavez?" "Um…yea… I've never seen it like this. I have seen suicides from drinking the acid.

It's a horrific way to die, and it's easy to get. I mean, dump the liquid out of a car battery, and you have the stuff. But someone went to great lengths to put it in a solid capsule that the digestive system could break down and then release in the stomach and small intestines. I sense that I'm not telling you anything you don't already know." John shook his head. Jade looked on as John rolled the balls around in the towel. Jade asked, "Homemade?" John nodded and said, "By someone who knows what the hell they are doing." Jade said, "Well, that's the cause of death. Someone fed this guy these things, and it had to be in the last few hours because there is no way they were in him any longer than that."

John nodded and looked at the clock over the morgue entrance. It was half past ten a.m. "I would guess he ate these between seven and eight, then give an hour for the body to start breaking down the 'candy coating,' and you get the release of the acid." Jade nodded and said, "It's a hell of a way to die, John. Someone hated this guy a whole lot." He just nodded as he handed the towel back to her. "Yea…a hell of a lot, Jade, a hell of a lot."

Howard Washington pulled up in front of the small tract home on Vanowen Street in Reseda at just before ten a.m. These were post world war two homes built in the late forties and mid-fifties. Modest lower income homes, all the same, three bedrooms, one bath, fourteen to sixteen hundred square feet. They jammed a lot of living into a really small space because of the post war housing boom.

This was also one very small part of the valley that the fires spared. Howard pulled the bike around the back and walked to the back door and knocked. There were some scurrying noises in the house, and then he heard the sound of one of the three deadbolt locks being released. The door opened, and he walked in.

There were two men sitting at a table in the small kitchen of the home. He said, "So, where is my breakfast?" The two Latino men called out in Spanish, and two young Latino girls walked in, nude. He

He threw the last girl to the floor and ordered them to be put in the prostitute rotation. "You only do in-house calls to men and women you know. The rest of the time it's out-calls only. I don't want anyone finding out about our business." He was zipping up his pants as the girls were taken into one of the small bedrooms where other girls were being raped. He looked out into the living room where ten men sat on sofas and chairs, waiting for their turn. He walked into the room in his uniform, and the faces of the all white older men dropped. "You never saw me. Just like I never saw you. Got it?" There were slow head nods around the room. Two were told their girls were ready, and they left the living room for the back bedrooms down a long hall.

Howard walked back into the kitchen and asked, "When does the next batch of girls come in?" "Two days." "How many?" "Ten." "All virgins?" "Si." "Okay. These seven are about used up for the house. Do you have arrangements for them as domestic sex slaves?" "Si." Howard was fixing his gun belt as he spoke, "Get me the list of the buyers, so I have it for my file. Are any of the girls going to Mr. El Compo?" "Si. Four." "Good, good, good. He is a great customer. He takes all of the girls, no matter what they look like or how hard we have used them, right?" "Si," said the second man who had been doing all of the conversing. Howard said, "Okay, well, I'm off. Make sure you call me when the new girls are in." The two men nodded their heads as Howard walked out the back door.

The crosshairs of the sniper rifle were trained on the back door of the house. Howard appeared in the doorway and the crosshairs after his tryst. He had a smile on his face and his helmet under his arm. He closed the door behind him. No one heard the shot, just the sound of Howard Washington's body hitting the ground on the back porch. The two men ran out the door to see what had happened. They didn't know it, but their heads were in the crosshairs of the sniper as well.

CHAPTER SEVEN

"Yea, like I'm the only fuckin'
guy here thinking that!"

J im was rounding his way down the 101 Freeway headed for Reseda and a homicide that had just been called in. He called John, who was in Northridge at the hospital, and told him that they had another homicide, and that it involved a cop and some others. John sped down Reseda Boulevard headed for the house, and Jim and John arrived at the same time. They met at the back door where three uniformed LAPD officers stood over the remains of the three men. Jim walked up and asked, "So, what the fuck do we have here?" "A mess!" He heard a voice from inside the home, a voice he knew all too well.

Jade Morgan stepped into the doorway, and Jim said, "Jesus Christ! Do you have fuckin' ESP now?" She laughed and said, "No...I was doing an autopsy for John at Northridge, and the call came over my radio. So, I drove right over. What a mess." John asked, "Do we have any idea who the guys are?" Jade said, "Well, the one in the police uniform has a name tag that says 'Washington' on it." John

and Jim looked at each other, and John pulled out his tablet and looked at the list from the Sanchez killing. "Son of a bitch," John said. Jade looked confused and asked, "What?"

John showed the tablet to Jim who nodded and said, "This fucker is on what we now know for certain is a hit list." "As in a hit man hit list?" Jade asked. They both nodded. "Well, if you come around to the front of the house, you will see why someone may have wanted to kill these guys."

The two men walked around the small house to find thirteen men in zip tie handcuffs sitting on the grass. All were white and middle-aged, and John didn't need to go inside to know what they were dealing with. He looked at Jade and asked, "Are there any fatalities?" She shook her head. "How many girls?" Jim asked. "Seven at last count and two boys."

Jim said, "Well, they just catered to all tastes, didn't they?" John and Jade shot him a dirty look, and Jim said, "Yea, like I'm the only fuckin' guy here thinking that!" John called for his CSI team and asked them to bring Steve Hoffman with them. Then he called immigration, and one of the officers on scene got really, really upset. He heard yelling, and he looked at Jade's face and knew who it was.

It took a few seconds, and Andre Espinoza appeared through the crowd of onlookers and police. "You're calling in immigration? Jesus, fuckin' feds. You assholes are always right there with that shit. These girls need to be treated and taken care of, and all you want to do is cart them off to some immigration station, so they can be packed up and shipped back across the border only to be grabbed again and returned here...or worse."

John's formidable frame towered over Espinoza who looked up to see John looking at him most disapprovingly. "They will be debriefed by my office before we turn them over to immigration, officer. You know the protocol."

Andre was clearly agitated seeing Swenson with Jade standing in the doorway behind him. He calmed down and said, "I want to talk to some of these victims and get their stories." John looked

on, confused, and asked, "What are you even doing here, Officer Espinoza? This is not anywhere near your patrol area?" "I'm off duty. I grew up only a few blocks from here. I was visiting my family when the call came in, so I came right over."

John asked, "Where does your family live?" Espinoza got a pissed off look on his face, and he glared at Jade. John said, "Why are you staring at Chief Medical Examiner Morgan? I don't think the answer to my question lies with her." Espinoza drew his eyes away from her and said, "My family lives at the corner of Wilbur and Heartland just off Vanowen." John said, "Literally right around the corner from the West Valley police station on Vanowen?" "Yea, so what? That's where I grew up, and I was first introduced to police work. The cops took me in when I was a kid. They kept me off the streets, and I became one of them. You got a problem with that?"

John shook his head slowly and said, "I was just curious how you got here so fast, that's all." Jim was watching the interaction between John, Andre, and Jade, and he knew that there was something wrong. "What the fuck's the deal here? You two have a love spat?" Jim asked with a bit of jest in his voice.

Andre turned to leave, and John asked, "Officer Espinoza? Would you be so kind as to wait a few moments? I would like to speak with you in private." "Go fuck yourself, Swenson. The FBI has no jurisdiction over me. No, I'm not going to wait around." He started to walk off, and John called out to one of his team members and said, "Please take Officer Espinoza into custody and hold him until I can speak with him."

Andre yelled out, "You can't do as you wish, you son of a bitch. I haven't done anything wrong. Fuck you. Fuck you!" He was combative when the agent took a hold of his arm and accidently belted the agent in the mouth. John saw it and made his way through the crowd to Andre, who was trying to help up the agent he struck. He felt a giant hand grab the back of his neck and his feet leave the ground. John flipped him around in his hands, holding Andre two feet off the ground and said, "You are now under arrest for assaulting a federal officer."

Andre's face went from anger to shame. John pulled him close and whispered into his face, "I'm the last man on the planet that you want to piss off, and you just did. You're under arrest, you son of a bitch." He put him down and cuffed him and took him to his truck. Jim watched the whole event unfold. He looked at Jade who was looking on with a look he didn't understand. Jim took out a cigarette from his left top pocket, lit it, and said to himself as he snapped the Zippo closed, "Interesting. I think it's going to get even more interesting for Officer Espinoza. Much, much more interesting."

John put Espinosa in the back of his truck and cuffed his feet as well. Steve wheeled up to him and said, "Are you done playing circle jerk, so we can process this crime scene?" John walked off with Steve wheeling next to him. They got near the back door where the bodies were now covered with a yellow tarp. "There's nothing to investigate here. This is the third police officer executed in order by an unknown assailant." Steve got a thoughtful look on his face and asked, "A serial killer?" John shook his head as Jim approached. "What's the topic of conversation that has John shaking his head?"

Steve looked up at Jim and said, "I asked John if we're dealing with a serial killer, and he shook his head." Jim laughed and handed Steve a bloodstained pamphlet that Jade had pulled off Washington's body. "The same as the others?" Steve asked. "You bet your fuckin' ass. This isn't a serial killer, boys. This is a hit man. We got us a cop killer, and he's really, really good."

John looked over at Espinoza sitting in the back of his truck. "Jim's right. This is not a serial killer. These are executions. Someone inside the LAPD has put a hit out on these people, and the killer knows all of their dirty little secrets."

Jim laughed. "I guess that's one way to clean up the department. I bet neither one of you has picked up on the pattern in these killings." John looked at Jim and said, "Outside of the damn list that the killer has supplied?"

Jim nodded. Steve looked on and said, "Well, Jim, what the fuck is the pattern?" "I have been checking these names out, and they don't come from Rampart division." Both John and Steve looked confused. "Not from

Rampart?" John asked. "Nope. All these mother fuckers come out of West Valley just down the street from here, and it gets better." "Really? How?" Steve asked. "That's where Garrison Cantrell originated as well." The look on John's face changed, and Jim caught it. "I just saw the light bulb come on in Agent Swenson's eyes." Steve said, "So, there's a hit man who's a cop who's gunning down cops and exposing their corruption?"

John nodded slowly. Steve motioned for the three men to come in close to his face. Steve said, "Um…isn't that what the Iron Eagle does?" John nodded slowly. Steve said, "But it's not the Eagle!" John and Jim nodded. "Well, gentlemen, we have a real problem because this isn't the Iron Eagle. And the Iron Eagle has no idea who it is, does he?" Steve was looking at John, who shook his head. "Well, we better get it figured out and fast before this guy expands his kills to us." With that, they broke off their private conversation. John walked back over to the crime scene and tapped Jade on the shoulder. She looked up and followed John to a corner of the house out of sight. "Are you oaky?" he asked. "No, John, I'm not okay. I think that you have the Iron Eagle in your truck. I think that Andre is the Eagle, and I think that is why he threatened me. Remember what the Eagle did to Barry Mullin and Jill Makin?"

John nodded. "Well? Shit, John. I think he's going to try to kill me." John put his hand on her trembling shoulder and said, "There are two things that I can promise you, Jade. First, I won't let him hurt you, and second, he's not the Iron Eagle." "How can you be so damn sure?" "Do you trust me?" She nodded. "Then trust me when I tell you that I am the foremost expert on the Iron Eagle, and Andre is not him. I think there is more to Andre than meets the eye, though, and I will get to the bottom of it." His hand was still on her shoulder, and he could feel the tension leaving her, and she stopped shaking. "Are you sure?" she asked. "Oh yes. I am a hundred percent sure. Now go back to work. From the blood stains, this is another sniper shot." She nodded, and the two walked back out from behind the house.

Jade went back to work, and Steve and John jumped in his truck with Andre in the back. Steve asked, "Where to?" "The office. We need to book Mr. Espinoza on federal assault charges and then have a chat.

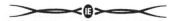

Garrison Cantrell finally got home at a little after three p.m. He walked into his home, and it was a mess. He had not been home since his arrest for Schultz's murder, and the cops tore the place apart looking for and, as far as he was concerned, planting evidence. He walked through the torn up remnants of his home and just shook his head. "Thanks a lot, guys. You really didn't have to fuck up my house." "That's what they do when they serve a search warrant!" Cantrell didn't respond right away. He just started picking things up and putting them back where they belonged. He finally acknowledged the male voice in the room. "To what do I owe the honor of a visit from you?" he said, putting items back on shelves. "You know why. So they let you out...how did you manage to get that accomplished?" "Does it matter?" "No...not really." "So what now?" Cantrell asked. He turned to see the short figure of a man in the shadow of his back door. "Well, I guess that all depends on you. What do you want to happen?"

Cantrell continued his cleanup and was uprighting his sofa when the man entered and helped him. Cantrell looked at him and said, "Alverez is dead. I got hung for that...I suppose that you are the one responsible for the killings in the past several days?" "Of course...but that's not news to you." Cantrell lifted up a love seat and sat down. He looked on at the man now standing in his living room, staying out of the line of sight of the front windows.

"With you under surveillance, your movements will be tracked. I helped Santone with the case law to get you out of jail. I have to do what I feel is best for myself and the protection of my business interests."

Cantrell was short tempered and asked, "What do you want? Do you want to know if I'm going to kill you?" "That would be a good start." "I'm not going to kill you." There was a pause, and the man asked, "Are you going to out the movement and what we are trying to accomplish?" Cantrell laughed. "Don't you think that if I was going to do that I would have done it a long time ago?" "Good point." "Thanks. So...why are you

here?" Cantrell asked. "You know why I'm here. You fell on the sword for a lot of men and women. You will be well compensated when this is over." "You're goddamn right I will be. I lost my career for you and your people. You're damn well going to pay me and pay me very, very well." "I will. I must be off. Keep your head down. You're on the FBI's radar. I saw Agents Swenson and Hoffman grab you after court. What did they want?"

Cantrell laughed. "Really nothing. They are clueless." "Don't underestimate Hoffman. He's been doing this a long time, and he knows who I am, and sooner or later, if he lives long enough, he's going to put two and two together." "So kill him." "Oh no…the plan is the plan, and we stick to it. This is about police corruption and nothing more." "And the Iron Eagle?" "Not a concern to us. He has no idea who we are or what we do. We are immune to his meddling."

Cantrell stood up and walked into the kitchen, passing the man. "Don't kid yourself. The Eagle is watching and looking, and if he gets a whiff of who might be involved, it will bring his wrath on everyone." "You let me worry about that. Just follow the court's instructions. You will be vindicated. We got Chavez and Washington today." "Well, you are moving right along." "That should be enough to get the charges against you dismissed. I will get a secret message to your attorney."

Cantrell sat down at the table in his kitchen and said, "These killing are only treating the symptoms; the disease is still rampant." "Yes, but that's where the Iron Eagle will come in. He will figure out the core problem and rid the city of it once and for all." "You're playing a dangerous game with the Eagle." "Well…it's what must be done." The man handed Cantrell a small satchel. "There is enough cash in here to last you a very, very long time. We will give you the all clear when we are finished." Cantrell just sat at the table with the satchel of cash as the man disappeared out the back door of his home. He sat looking at the stacks of money and said, "I think you're wrong. I think the Iron Eagle is going to get you all." He was talking to empty air as he packed the cash back into the bag and continued cleaning up the mess.

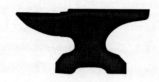

CHAPTER EIGHT

*"What do you know about
these cop killings?"*

Steve and John made it back to the office with Espinoza in tow. They sent him up to booking, and when he was finished there, he was sent down to an interrogation room on John's floor. When John got the call, he buzzed Steve that Espinoza was ready to be interviewed.

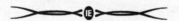

"Well, Howard certainly fucked things up, didn't he?" Marco Estrada was sitting in the plush Beverly Hills estate of Mark El Compo. El Compo handed him a drink and continued, "I mean, the fucker was a sick and sadistic bastard and deserved to die. I just wish he hadn't been killed on one of my properties…and just when I have several shipments of women and drugs coming into the country."

"It will have no impact, sir. I have everything worked out with customs. Nothing will go wrong. All I need to know is where you

want the girls. The drugs already have a home, and there is a silver lining to Howard's death." "Oh really?" El Compo said. "Yes, sir, there is. You can now offer virgins to your customers. You don't have that asshole screwing them up. Man, he tore the shit out of the last two girls before he was killed. I heard one of my people at the hospital say that while vaginas and anuses can take a pounding and retain their shape, Washington really trashed both girls' throats. They would have been of no use for oral pleasure for your customers."

El Compo laughed and said, "You're really wrong on the throat issue. Howard did cost me money on selling virgins, and, yes, they do fetch a better price. But what he did to all of the girls he forced himself on orally was the best thing to happen to them for the sex trade. When he was done with them, they had no gag reflex, and they could take any size man. Here, I will show you."

El Compo called out two names, and the two women walked into the room, nude. He was sitting in a satin robe and opened it to reveal a large boner. "Take out your cock." Estrada pulled his pants down, and El Compo ordered the two girls to perform oral sex on them. When they were finished, they stood up and wiped the sides of their mouths and smiled. "You see? No gag reflex. No matter what the angle, Howard did do me a service there."

He sent the women off to prepare his meal and said, "I would invite you to join me, but I know you have other work to attend to. Have the ten girls coming in this week taken to my house in Woodland Hills. It has been rebuilt, and there are no neighbors to deal with. I want you to break them. It won't take much, then I want you to use them for out calls only. Let's keep the johns away from my properties for a while." They shook hands, and El Compo said, "Cantrell has been dealt with. He's on pretrial release and GPS tracking." Marco laughed and said, "Really? You really think that he has been dealt with? That will only happen when there's a bullet in his head." El Compo said, "I have been to his house, and we have talked. He will be compensated for his fall. There's nothing to worry about from him." Marco just laughed as he walked out the door.

John walked down the hall to get Steve and found him asleep in his chair. He walked up and checked his pulse, and it was strong, but his breathing was labored. He stood for a moment and then pressed firmly on Steve's shoulder, and he woke up. "Oh, John, shit. Did I fall asleep?" "Yea...it's been a rough day. Are you sure you want to be in on the Espinoza interview?" "Yes. I have a feeling that Espinoza knows way more than we think." John wheeled him into the interrogation room. When they arrived, Espinosa was clearly shaken. "Look, John, I didn't mean to strike your agent. It was an accident." "Yes...of course, an accident. Tell me about you and Jade Morgan?" Andre had a surprised look on his face as if he didn't think John knew that there was a relationship. "There's nothing to tell. We're friends with benefits." John sat back in a chair across from Andre and said, "Yea...I'm not clear on that. Want to elaborate a little more?"

Andre was getting angry, and he asked, "Did you assholes arrest me so you can dig into my love life?" John laughed as did Steve. Steve said, "No, Andre, we don't give a flying fuck about your love life. We want to know what you were doing on that crime scene." "I already answered that question."

John sat back and put his arms behind his head. He had changed out of his suit and was in an FBI polo shirt and jeans. Andre just stared at his huge arms. "You did and you didn't, Andre," John said, "I pulled your call logs, and you were on duty. You called a code for lunch, and you were a hell of a long way from East LA. Now, I'm not a lunch expert, but I do know that a guy on duty doesn't drive some thirty plus miles from his patrol turf home for lunch. I mean, what are you? A mama's boy?" Andre was defiant, "I answered the question. I had a two-hour break, and I went over to see my folks. I was on the record, and my whole day up to the call to the crime scene is logged. Unless you forgot, my patrol car has a GPS tracker in it, so the department knows where my car is at any moment."

John nodded and asked, "Do you know Officer Garrison Cantrell?" There was a moment of silence. "Um...do I know him? No. Have I heard

of him? Yea, of course. The dude got railroaded out of the department for breaking the law." "You would never do that, would you Officer Espinoza…break the law, I mean?" Steve asked coldly. "No…my job is to uphold the law and protect the people of Los Angeles." John asked, "You were a sniper in the Army, isn't that correct?" Andre remained defiant. "What? Did you pull my fuckin' background and military records?" "Yes!" "Yea, I was a sharp shooter in the Army, and I was a sniper in the field." "You saw a lot of action in Afghanistan and Iraq." "Yea…that was a long time ago. I've been a civilian and a cop for nearly five years." John put his hands down on the table and said, "Yes, I know that." He pointed to Steve and said, "We know that. What we don't understand is what you were doing on a crime scene where a police officer and two others had their heads blown off by a sniper."

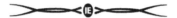

It was near sundown, and Patricia Salazar walked out of one of the makeshift trailers at the West Valley branch of the LAPD. She had been a detective in internal affairs for nearly a decade and had a reputation as a brutal investigator and a man hater. Part of that was a result of her merciless attack on the men in her department, and the other was her long-time openly lesbian relationship with Mary Schultz. The comments around the department since Schultz's murder were that Salazar was gunning for anyone. She walked out to her unmarked sedan, popped the trunk, dropped her bag and laptop inside, and drove out of the parking lot, destination unknown. What Pat didn't know was that she wasn't alone, and the blinking light of the GPS signal from her car was reading strongly in the car that was following at a great distance.

She stopped at a well-known gay bar at the corner of Vanowen and Tampa, parked, and walked in. Her pursuer followed the blinking light and parked across the street from the bar and waited. Patricia was greeted immediately by several friends that she and Mary were involved with. She joined them for a drink and some quiet conversation until one of the ladies

asked, "So, do you want to take out your frustrations?" Patricia swigged the shot of bourbon in her glass and said, "Fuck yes!" "Well, then, follow me."

It was Chris Alton who had made the invitation, and she and Patricia walked back to a red door at the back of the bar that led into a private club. They knocked, and the bouncer inside slid a panel on the door to see who was there. Patricia said, "It's like going into a speakeasy in the twenties during prohibition." Chris laughed as the door opened, and they entered the underground club. The name said it all, 'House of Pain,' in red neon, nearly the only light in the dimly lit room painted in red and black. The two sat down in a black leather booth, and the bartender walked over and gave them another drink.

Patricia was very well-known in the club, and they keep a very, very select group of slaves just for her. Mary used to be her slave in the bondage and S&M club, but since her death Pat didn't want role play anymore. She wanted to inflict pain on innocent victims. The club specialized in human trafficking, mostly Asians, and since they were plentiful, they were also disposable, which allowed an elite group of clients to inflict pain on those sold into servitude.

Pat slugged down her shot and walked into one of the dressing rooms off the main floor. There were six doors, each went to a different dungeon. All were soundproof, and the staff of the club cleaned up the mess. She stripped down nude and put on a pair of thigh high leather boots with stiletto heels, a pair of crotchless leather panties, and nothing more. She walked into the dungeon where two young Asian men laid nude on two Saint Andrew's Cross boards facing each other. She walked in and took down a whip and stood in between the two men. Waving the whip over her head in a profane and professional manner, she struck each man as she moved with grace in her opening of torture.

Her long blond hair went down to the middle of her back, and for a woman of sixty, she had a great body. She walked between the men, forcing them to pleasure her as she moved the cross into the positions that she desired with a remote. Both men were gagged with ball gags. The red balls in their mouths had been modified; they were steel not

plastic, and the head restraints that held them in place were spiked on the inside. It kept the ball in the mouth of the victim while causing excruciating pain as the steel spikes dug into their skulls.

Small trickles of blood were running down both of the boy's faces as she worked on them. She attached weights to their testicles, one on each ball, and when she raised the cross, the weight pulled down on their scrotum, causing them to scream through the gag. The more pain she inflicted, the more excited and brutal she became. She pierced each man's penis with a hot steel rod, then removed it, reheated it, and rammed it up their urethras where it smoked and sizzled. All the while, the helpless men could only scream.

She took inch and a half injection needles and passed them through each man's nipples and scrotum, working in a lattice pattern, tying their balls together with a string on the needles, and when she was finished with her crafting, she ripped the needles out of the nipples and scrotum at the same time.

One of the bouncers called out to her over a loud speaker that it was two a.m. She would need to wrap things up because it was closing time. She removed each man from the cross and tied them on their knees to a leather bench. She tied their necks to the bench and their ankles together with a strap across their mid section.

She grabbed a three foot two inch pole and lubricated it good then drove it up through the anus of the first boy. He let out a yelp through the gag, and she grabbed a long, hard board and, with great strength, used it like a hammer to drive the pole deeper and deeper into the kid until he was dead. The other boy watched in horror as blood began to run out of the other's mouth, and his pupils began to dilate.

She walked over to the other and said, "It's your turn to please me, my boy," and she repeated the process. When she was finished, she took a shower in the bath provided and finally left the club a little after three a.m. with Chris. The two walked out into the dimly lit parking lot, and Chris asked, "Does my dominatrix want to take this party to my place?" Pat nodded and got in Chris's car, and the two sped off to

Chris's home just a few blocks from the club. Chris spent the rest of the night pleasing Pat and doing her bidding, knowing she had gotten the desire to kill out of her system…for at least that night.

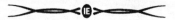

Steve and John had finished interrogating Andre and remanded him to the custody of the U.S. Marshal's office in the federal building. He had begged to be released, but John told him that he had to face a federal judge at the courthouse on the charges he had been arrested on. It was nearly ten p.m. when Steve and John left the office for home. As they drove down PCH to Malibu, Steve asked, "So…do you think he's the sniper?" John never took his eyes off the road while answering, "I think he is one of them." Steve looked out the window and struggled to take a deep breath and said, "You think there are more?" "Yes…I think this goes way beyond the police force itself. I think that a few officers are doing some house cleaning but not for the betterment of the department. I think it is to raise their fellow officers through the ranks to strengthen their position." "What the hell kind of position would that be?" "A crime syndicate that can move with impunity through LA, trafficking in drugs, guns, humans. You name it." "That's it? A few bad cops are doing all this to make even more cops bad?" "Yep…but in order to do it they are going to have to kill at least six more high ranking officials, and I have to figure out how to stop them." "YOU or the Eagle?" John looked over at Steve for a moment and said, "For the first time in my career, and in the life of the Eagle, I can't tell where the line is."

Steve started to shake his head slowly and said, "Remember that slippery slope I told you about regarding keeping your work separate from the Eagle's?" John nodded. "Well, you're sliding down it. You better get it sorted out really, really fast, John, because if the Iron Eagle and John Swenson become one and the same…you will get caught, and you will die."

John nodded as they pulled up to the main entrance of the house. John helped Steve into his wheelchair, and Steve sat up and said, "I'm having trouble breathing." "I'll take you to Sara. She will know what to do." He headed toward the main house, and Steve said, "I feel my time is starting to run out, John. We need to solve this case. It's the last case that I'm going to work on. If I die before it gets resolved, you could end up lost." John didn't say anything. He just wheeled Steve into the house and woke Sara who took Steve to one of the operating rooms.

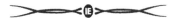

Karen Faber had finished a seventy-two hour shift and was getting ready to leave the hospital for the night when a patient she had seen a few days earlier stopped her in the hall. He was a nice looking young man, she figured in his early twenties, and he asked if he could buy her a drink. She laughed and said, "That's very sweet of you, but I don't drink. It's also after closing time for most restaurants and bars. It's almost three a.m." Her prospective suitor would not be dissuaded and asked her on a date. "I tell you what…Marco, right?" He nodded. "I will go out with you but not tonight. Why don't you give me a call?" She took out her prescription pad and wrote her cell phone number on it and handed it to him. "Call me tomorrow, and we will set up a time to have lunch…agreed?"

Marco Estrada had been in the ER when Gilbert was brought in. He had come in as an unconnected patient, though he wanted to make sure that Gil died, and in the act of doing that was smitten with Karen. "Okay, Doctor Faber. I will give you a call tomorrow afternoon, so I make sure you get a good night's sleep." She nodded, and he asked if she needed a ride. She told him that she had her own car, and he offered to walk her to it. She smiled and said, "That would be nice. I would feel much safer having a police escort." Marco smiled and said, "A beautiful woman like you should have twenty-four seven police protection, and if I have anything to say about it that's what you're going to get." They shared a laugh as they exited the hospital and headed for the parking structure.

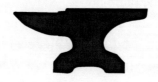

CHAPTER NINE

"You know what the Eagle once told me?
'The early cop gets the corpse.'"

The house was quiet when Jim walked in after two a.m. He knew that Barbara would be asleep, or so he thought. He reset the alarm and saw a light on at the far end of the house. He walked down to the living room, and the patio doors were open, and Barbara was sitting in a lounge chair with her feet in the pool. It was high tide, and the sound of the sea pounding against the rocks far below the cliffside home they had built almost drowned out his voice. "Good morning!" he said in a loud voice. Barbara jumped, throwing her drink in the air. "Jesus Christ, Jimmy. Are you trying to give me a fuckin' heart attack? Shit. My fuckin' scotch is all over me. Where the hell have you been?" She removed her robe, exposing her nude skin, and walked over and filled her glass with ice and scotch and poured one for Jim.

"I'm sorry, Barb. I didn't know if you could hear me over the surf." He took the drink from her with a thank you and threw himself

down on the couch. "Where the fuck have I been? I've been in a fuckin' nightmare that's where I've been. We got a killer out there, Barb, and he's going to be one tough son of a bitch to catch."

Barbara sat down on the couch next to him, nude, and asked, "What about the Eagle?" Jim shook his head. "I don't know. I think the Eagle might be losing his touch. He hasn't made a move or even attempted one. We all met today, and he doesn't have a clue." "What about you, Jimmy? Do you have a clue?" "All I know for sure is that there is a hit man or hit men that are targeting high level LAPD officers and killing them. Don't get me wrong. So far, none of the people killed were in any way innocent. They all had their own baggage and their own bad stuff." Barbara took a drink of her scotch and said, "It sounds like the type of people the Eagle goes after." "Yea...I think that's the problem. This is internal police corruption, and I think that it has the Eagle stumped. I know I am."

Barb took another drink and asked, "Didn't you tell me that the killings are in some sort of order?" He nodded. She looked at him for a few seconds and then hit him on the top of his head with her glass. "Hey, dumb ass...did it occur to you to stake out the next person on the list?" "Do you think I'm a moron? Yea, it fuckin' occurred to me. Ouch! That hurt. You might have given me brain damage." Barbara started laughing. "In order to give you brain damage, you have to have a brain to damage, which, obviously, you don't. So why are you sitting here? Get your ass out to the next victim's home and see what's going on."

Jim swigged down the last drink of his scotch. He looked at the clock, and it was half past three. "You're right, goddamn it, but I'm not going alone." He pulled his cell phone out and called John. "Swenson." "Are you asleep?" "Am I talking to you?" "Yep!" "Then how the hell can I be asleep? What's up?" "Barbara just gave me a brilliant idea. Let's stake out the home of the next person on the list and see what happens." "It's after three a.m.!" "You know what the Eagle once told me? 'The early cop gets the corpse.'" Jim let out a laugh, and John could hear Barbara laughing, too. "Funny, really fuckin' funny."

John pulled out his tablet while sitting in the living room. Sara was still with Steve. "Okay, next one on the list is Patricia Salazar." There was a moment of silence, and he heard Jim tell Barbara who was next. There was some murmuring on the other end of the line, and John asked, "Are you talking to Barbara about an active case?" "Yep, and she just told me if it's Salazar, let the killer have the sick psycho bitch." John sat up and asked to speak to Barbara.

"Hi John boy!" "Hello Boobra…you know Salazar?" "Yes I do, and she is one crazy ass bitch with a real mean streak." "How do you know her?" "Jill and I played a little in the BDSM world; you do know what that is, right?" "Yes, Barbara, I know about bondage and sadomasochism." "Good. Anyway, Jill and I tried it out, and it wasn't our thing, but Jill had the misfortune of having Patricia as her dom in a role play a couple of years before she was murdered. The woman really hurt her. She told me that she ignored all of her safe words and beat the living shit out of her. I remember that Jill said when she was freed, before the bitch could put her into another position, she tackled her and beat the hell out of her. She and her lover, Mary Schultz, were into some deep, dark, sick, twisted shit. They were into some under-underground clubs, if you know what I mean." "Yes. I know exactly what you mean. Human trafficking."

Barbara laughed a serious laugh and said, "More like human torture and murder trafficking. The kind of people who never show up on a radar. As I recall, they were really into Asian men…they were both doms in the clubs, but Mary was the sub at home." John asked, "Do you recall any of the clubs that you went to?" Barbara paused before saying, "We went to several with them, but the club that threw us over the edge was called the 'House of Pain.' I don't remember the name of the bar, but it's located at the corner of Vanowen and Tampa in Reseda in the San Fernando Valley. Do you know where I'm talking about?" "Yes, yes I do. It's only a few blocks from the West Valley Police Station." "Oh yea, that's right. Patricia is a detective in internal affairs out there. That station was destroyed in the fires, wasn't it?"

John was quiet for a second and then answered, "Um…yes, but they are rebuilding, and they have some mobile buildings on the land, so they can operate out there." "Well, I hope that helps you." "It does, Barb, it does. Put Jim back on."

Jim got on the line, and John said, "You go to Salazar's home. I'm going to check out this club that Barbara told me about." Jim asked, "Are you checking it out or is the Eagle?" "I will know when I get there." Jim hung up and looked at Barbara and said, "You sure know how to light a fire under a man's ass." "Well, I've been fucked up the ass enough by you. I should know by now!" He kissed her on the lips and told her he wasn't going to be getting any sleep. She looked at him and said, "You sleep less now than when you were a detective. When is this sheriff shit over with?" "The election is the end of this year, and once the people decide, I am so fuckin' out of there." Barbara had a nervous look on her face and sound to her voice, "That's a long way off, Jimmy. Just don't get killed before your term ends." He walked out the door headed for Salazar's home.

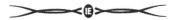

John walked back to the lair and took out a couple of gym bags of equipment and his body armor. Sara saw him in the office putting things together. "Is the Eagle on the prowl?" "I don't know yet. How's Steve?" I have him on oxygen. I want to bring Gail over to be with him. Is that all right?" "Can you take him back to his house? I don't want her knowing my alter ego." "He's comfortable. I would rather let him rest here for a few hours before he moves. I don't think you have anything to fear from Gail. Remember what her ex does?" John nodded and said, "The Hudson River Killer. For a few moments, I forgot. Yea, it's fine. Bring her over but keep her out of the conference room. If she asks why, tell her it's for private patients." Sara laughed. "Yea, she'll buy that." She kissed John on the cheek and told him to be careful. He looked at her face and asked, "Is Steve in any immediate danger?" "No…honey. He's just winded. The ALS

is progressing. This is going to get more and more frequent until he has to make the call to end his life." John looked on and said, "I hope he gets to go out his own way and not from that damn disease." She nodded and watched as he walked out the door.

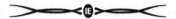

Patricia woke just after six, a few minutes before Chris's alarm was to go off. It was still dark with just a hint of sunlight on the horizon. She sat up in bed. Neither had anything covering them, and she nudged Chris and told her to go down on her. Pat spread her legs while Chris did as she was told. Pat lit a cigarette while Chris ate her out. Chris looked up and saw the cherry of the smoke in Pat's mouth as she took a drag off it in the dark room. Chris spoke as she licked, "Pat, please don't put that out on my back." Pat took another drag off the cigarette and said, "Did I give you permission to speak? Eat!"

Chris did as instructed and worked hard to get Pat off, but she watched Pat's body language as the sun began to rise and light the bedroom, and she could see that Pat wasn't even paying attention to the pleasure she was trying to give her. She watched as Pat took the last hit off the cigarette, the red hot tip ablaze, and as she expelled the smoke from her lungs, she reached forward and stubbed out the cigarette on Chris's back. She winced in pain but said nothing and just kept licking as Pat lit another cigarette. The room was well lit by the time Pat was through with the second smoke, and she looked down into Chris's eyes and saw the tears and the hopeless surrender to the continued and inevitable pain. Pat smiled as she stubbed out the second one on her back and lit another.

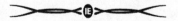

Jim pulled up near Salazar's home a little after five a.m. He looked around, but there was no car there and no lights on. He looked for any

other cars, but there were none. He took a cigarette out of his left top pocket and flipped open his Zippo and lit it. He took a deep hit of the smoke and waited for movement.

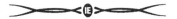

John pulled his Silverado into the parking lot of Pete's Place, the gay bar that Barbara had told him about, and pulled out his tablet. There was one car in the lot, and he ran the plate. It came back as being an LAPD unmarked car. The LAPD had a long standing radio transmitting code, KMA-365. It was common for staff and family members to have it on a license plate frame to show they were affiliated with the LAPD. But most people don't know that LAPD officers have their own unique KMA call sign, which is used for internal identification of an active duty officer. John ran the car and its VIN number through the federal database, which can ID any vehicle in the national databases, and he got the person assigned to the car, Detective Patricia Salazar of the LAPD West Valley Division.

It was six fifteen, still pretty dark, and the lot was not lit. He got out of the truck and walked up to the vehicle. There was nothing out of the ordinary, and he was about to walk back to his truck when he heard a faint beeping sound. It was really, really light. Most people would not even hear it. It took a trained ear, and he had one. He had his tablet in his hand, and he bent down beside the driver's side of the car and placed the tablet with its infrared camera on it under the frame. He ran the length of the car, pulled out the tablet, and looked at the images. Near the rear of the driver's side frame, he saw a larger than usual GPS transmitter, and he knew that it was not LAPD. It had been placed there. He typed several commands into his tablet and was able to triangulate a reverse directory of the signal and identify that it was being picked up by a receiver a half-mile away.

The Eagle pulled his black body armor from the truck and dressed quickly. He took off following the green blip until he passed it on Tampa. He looked around the now slightly lit street as the sun was rising and the streetlights were going out. He parked on the other side

of the street from the blip on his tablet, grabbed a GPS tracker from his bag, typed some coordinates into it using a split screen, and left the truck. He followed the green icon until it showed he was standing in front of the vehicle. The Eagle could see a head laying on the head rest of the car, and he slipped the GPS unit under the car frame until he felt it grab. He held it tight as not to allow it to make the sharp clicking noise that the magnet usually makes when attaching. With the GPS in place, he took a picture of the license plate and moved back to his truck. He ran the plate, and it came back as an LAPD unmarked car. He ran the KMA number, only this time it came back classified.

The sun was rising, and he could see the person in the car. He backed up his truck and took several photographs of the occupant. He knew he could not process and analyze them on scene, but he could at the office. He was just getting ready to pull out to leave when the car started moving. The Eagle sat and watched as the car pulled out and began to move down the street in the direction of Pete's Place. When the car was out of sight, he turned his truck around, without lights, and followed the car slowly down Tampa. The car parked at the corner of Tampa and Vanowen on the opposite side of the street from the bar. The Eagle drove on past swiftly and turned onto the first street directly across from the bar's parking lot. He watched as a female approached the car and then entered. He saw her motion to turn the key, and, instantly, there was a violent explosion.

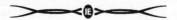

Jim was only two blocks away and half asleep in his car when he heard the explosion. He looked around and saw a fireball rising into the air. He pulled onto the street and headed for the source of the blast. The concussion from the blast blew out windows and set off car alarms for blocks. He called in a code to dispatch, but he heard the sirens in the distance before he ever got the call out. He got out of his car and started to cross the street when a dark sedan gunned its engine and headed straight for him. He moved as quickly as he could to get out of the way, but the car was veering

in his direction. He realized that the car was trying to hit him. He dropped to the ground and rolled toward the gutter when he heard another vehicle screeching its tires in his direction. The sedan was racing up Tampa toward the 101 Freeway, and hot on its tail was a Silverado pickup truck.

He pulled himself up on his hands and knees just as firefighters, an ambulance, and police arrived on scene. One of the officers recognized Jim and got to him and helped him up. "Are you all right, Sheriff?" Jim was wiping small pieces of glass out of his hands from the street near the bar as he answered, "Yea…yea…fuck…I'm fine. Whoever's in that car is dead. Clear the building." The firemen were dowsing the flames of Patricia's car as he called for his CSI team. The street cop looked at him and asked, "Why do you want to clear the bar? It's closed and no one's around." Jim took out a cigarette and tapped it on his wrist then put it in his mouth and lit it. "The bar might be closed, but I guarantee you it ain't empty."

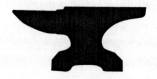

CHAPTER TEN

*"I promise you will beg for death
long before you will ever taste it."*

T he race was on as the sedan ripped up Tampa headed for the 101
Freeway with the Eagle in hot pursuit. The earliness of the morning
made it easier as there was little to no traffic. "I've got to cut him
off before he gets to the freeway!" the Eagle said as he raced down
Tampa. The LA River basin ran alongside the street, and the Eagle knew
if he could do a pit maneuver on the sedan at Victory, he could push him
right over the side of the basin. He was right on the sedan's tail as the
two entered the intersection, and the Eagle turned the wheel hard to the
right and caught the sedan's rear bumper perfectly. It slid sideways, and
the Eagle stayed against the bumper until the sedan made an evasive
maneuver and crashed through the gates of the LA River basin.

As the sedan slid down the side of the wash and into the basin, the
Eagle kept hitting its rear end. The driver was definitely well trained and
recovered after each hit. They headed toward a bridge abutment, and
the Eagle took full advantage, driving the truck hard into the sedan and

sending it into an uncontrollable spin. The car hit the concrete abutment on the passenger side door then spun to the right, flipped, and rolled.

The Eagle followed until the car stopped rolling and ended up on its tires. He could hear the driver trying to restart the car. The Eagle drove his truck into the driver's side door, pinning the driver inside. The Eagle pulled on his mask and stepped out of the truck. The driver of the sedan let out a volley of bullets. Two struck the Eagle in the chest, but he didn't flinch. The sedan's windshield was partially intact, so the Eagle smashed out the remaining glass and reached for the occupant. He got a hold of the dark figure and pulled him from the car. The driver was wearing a ski mask. The Eagle swatted him on the back of the neck, dropping him to his knees, zip tied his hands, pulled out a tranquillizer gun, and shot the driver in the shoulder. Seconds later, the driver fell over. The Eagle picked him up and threw him in the back of his truck. He walked over to the car and removed the GPS transmitter and grabbed a black case that was on the floor of the sedan. He jumped into his truck and made his way out of the basin and on to Malibu.

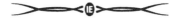

Karen woke a little after nine a.m. She walked through the house, but it was empty. Her mother and father had gone off to their offices, both were in private practice. She went to the kitchen to make breakfast. She threw a couple of eggs into a bowl and covered it with a paper towel and microwaved them with some bacon. She walked out onto the patio and sat down near the pool at the picnic table that her folks used for entertaining and ate her breakfast and drank a Coke, a habit she had picked up from her godfather, John Swenson. She was just settling in for a little rest when her phone rang. The caller ID was unidentified, and she was going to ignore it but decided she better answer. "Hello!" "Hi, Karen, it's Sara. I'm sorry to bother you on your day off, but I wanted to let you know that the autopsy report on the detective that came in yesterday is in."

Karen took a drink of her soda and asked, "So did we kill him?" "No, of course not. He was poisoned. I'm sending the reports over to John for Jade, but I wanted you to know." There was a moment of silence and Karen asked, "What kind of poison could do that kind of damage without the person knowing they ingested it?" "It's not anything I have ever seen before. The poison is sulfuric acid, and the way it was ingested was through a breakfast food."

Karen looked down at her eggs and asked, "What kind of breakfast food?" "The detective was able to get the word burrito out before he died. I can only guess that he ate a breakfast burrito, but from where I have no idea." She put the paper towel back over her eggs and said, "Um…thanks for the call. You just killed my appetite." "Sorry about that. Enjoy your days off." Sara was going to hang up when Karen called out to her, "Sara, before you go, can I ask you a question?" "Sure. What's up?" "I'm being courted by a police officer who was in the ER yesterday at the same time that that detective came in. He's a nice looking man but at least ten years older than me."

Sara asked quite clearly, "Does he know that you're seventeen?" "No!" "Well, you look older, you act older, and you are educated far beyond other women your age. But my dear, you are still under eighteen, and that makes physical contact with you illegal. You are not emancipated, and you still live with your folks." "So, if I tell him my age, will he go away?" Sara laughed. "You can tell him your age, but I doubt that it will make him go away. Just let him know. That way he's informed. And don't have sex with him. You and he will get into a lot of trouble."

Karen burped from the Coke, and Sara said, "Please tell me that you're not taking after John?" "I can't help it. It's what's for breakfast. Some people have coffee or tea. I have Coke!" Sara laughed and asked, "Oh…did you get the officer's name?" "Yea…Marco Estrada. Do you know him?" "No, but John might. You might want to give him a call and let him know. You know how protective he is of you." "Will do. Don't work too hard." They said quick goodbyes and hung up.

Karen pulled the paper towel off her eggs and said, "There is no poison in this. I made it for God's sake." She dug into her breakfast while enjoying the late morning sunshine and the warmth of the sun on her face. Afterwards, she picked up her cell and called John.

"Swenson." "Hello, Mr. Angel." A smile broke across his face as he looked on at the sleeping man in the rear of his truck. "To what do I owe this phone call from my best kid doctor?" Karen took another sip of her soda and heard John laugh. "What?" she asked. "It's ten a.m., and you're drinking a Coke, aren't you?" "Yes...Sara was mad at me." "Yea, well, welcome to the club. What's going on, honey?" "Jade told me that the detective we worked on yesterday died from poisoning. She said it was sulfuric acid."

"Yea...I knew about that yesterday. Jade handed me some of the pellets used to kill him." "Pellets?" "Glass units used to deliver the lethal dose of acid. They're soft enough that you can eat them but not so soft that they'll break in your mouth. It's an old way of killing someone. They break down in the digestive system, and the acid eats its way out. That's why the detective bled out. I know you didn't call me to talk forensics." "No. Sara told me to give you a call and ask you about a police officer who likes me. To see if you know him." "You do know you're seventeen, so even if you like the guy, you can't date him or have sex." "Yes, yes, papa bear. Sara read me the riot act."

"So, what's the officer's name?" "Marco Estrada." There was silence on the other end of the line but only momentarily. "How did you meet Officer Estrada?" "He was in the ER yesterday at the same time as the detective that died. I saw him after Sara and I had closed the case, and he was hanging around the hospital when I went home this morning." "What time did you see him as a patient?" "Oh, John, there is no way I can remember that. It was early in the day for sure." "What time did you run into him this morning?" "It was well after two a.m. I was coming off shift, and there he was. I gave him my cell number after he asked me out, then he walked me to my car." "Did you tell him your age?" She laughed. "No...he's cute, and I didn't want to scare him off. Do you know him?"

"Yes, Karen, in a sense. I know who he is, and I have had some interaction with him." "So, is he a good guy, bad guy? Can I talk to him and tell him my age and maybe have lunch with him at the hospital cafeteria?" "I would rather that you not hang out with him. I'm not saying he's a good guy, bad guy, or anything else. You're seventeen, and you won't be eighteen for almost a year. Stick to your practice of medicine. There will be plenty of time for boys, men, when you're legal."

"You're just mad because I'm jail bait!" John laughed. "No. I'm trying to protect you and Officer Estrada. Even when men know your age, they don't always take no for an answer." "They do when I tell them that my godfather is John Swenson of the FBI." "You didn't tell that to Estrada, did you?" "No…the conversation never got that far. Why? Do you want me to?" "No…tell him your age and that you're flattered and leave it alone. If he doesn't leave you be, then you call me, and I will take care of it. Understood?" "Yes, sir." "Sara told me you're off for a couple of days," said John. "Yep." "Why don't you come by the house tomorrow. I think Sara is going to be off, and we can all get together. I haven't seen you in months." "That sounds like fun. What time?" John said his calendar was clear and recommended that they meet after noon. "I will put it in my phone now," Karen said, "and I will be at your house tomorrow afternoon." "Okay, kid. Keep up the good work." "I will, John…" She paused briefly and said, "John?" "Yes." "You know that I know who you really are, don't you?" "Yes. I'm your godfather." Karen paused again before saying, "I love you." "I know that, sweetheart, and I love you, too. See you tomorrow." John hung up the phone and looked down at the list of victims laying in the passenger seat. He pointed to Brian Boyd's name and said, "You are next. I need to get to you first."

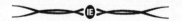

Jim was standing with U.S. Immigration, Steve Hoffman, and Jade Morgan at the bar where he had discovered a human sex trafficking ring. There were two holding rooms for the prisoners. One was a dank,

dark room with mattresses on the floor where the men and women satisfied customers. The other was a refrigerated unit that held the bodies of those killed in the dungeon. Most were young Asian men, but there were a few women as well.

Jim looked at Jade and Steve and said, "This club was a women's only club and, for the most part, catered to the lesbian community." Jade quickly corrected him, saying, "Jim, this is not a part of the lesbian lifestyle. This is a sick, twisted, fetish club that has nothing to do with being gay, lesbian, straight, or anything else. These people have been imported to feed a need to inflict pain and torture, the type rarely allowed by even the most submissive of partners."

Jim nodded in agreement. Steve just looked on. "How did you get down here, Steve?" Jim asked. "John sent one of the field agents to pick me up and bring me. I had a hard night." Jim didn't say anything nor did Jade. Steve asked, "On that note, where is John?" Jim looked on and said, "I think he had some personal business to attend to." Jade said, "Well, I don't know what can be more personal than the killing of yet another police officer." Jim asked, "How the hell could you know that any of these people are cops?" Jade frowned and said, "The car, dumb ass. The woman in the car was a detective with the West Valley division named Patricia Salazar." Steve and John looked at each other and scanned a copy of the list from the killer. They both pulled out pens and crossed her name off. Jade saw what they were doing and asked, "What do you two have?" "A list of the people to be killed. This is number five of a total of ten on the hit list." Steve wheeled himself over to the door to the parking lot, and Jim followed. Jade went back to the cooler to continue her work.

Jim walked up behind Steve and pushed the chair out the door into the light of day. "What's on your mind, Steve?" Jim asked. "The Eagle has the killer, doesn't he?" Jim said, "I don't know. He was chasing him. I saw his truck tailing another car that was trying to run me down as I approached the scene right after the explosion."

Steve wheeled himself over to the burnt out remains of the car and looked at it carefully. Jim stood and watched as Steve called for a crime

scene kit and gloves. He took a swab from one of the packets and wiped some material off the lower part of the car's frame. Jim asked, "What you got?" "C4. Whoever created this device wanted to make damn sure that the person in the car died." Jim laughed and said, "Well, they accomplished their mission because that bitch is dead!" "Strong words there, Jim. Did you know her?" Steve asked. "No, but Barbara did, and she said that she was a cruel and sadistic bitch." Steve looked on at the burned out wreck. "She might have been all those things, but she died painlessly. She never even heard the explosion." Jim nodded, knowing that it's the way Steve wanted to go — fast and painless.

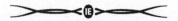

The Eagle pulled his truck into the underground tunnel leading to his lair. He pulled the man from the back of his truck and flung him over his shoulder. Once inside, he strapped the man to a gurney in one of the operating rooms. He filled a syringe with a stimulant and injected the masked man through his clothes. The Eagle pulled off the mask, and he recognized the man immediately.

Alberto Alverez was bleeding from cuts over his mouth and left eye. "You're a dead man," the Eagle said, looking Alverez in the eyes. "So I've been told. Am I to assume I'm in the company of the Iron Eagle?" The Eagle nodded. "It's nice to meet you," Alverez said, "I know you're going to torture and kill me, but I can tell you that you will get no information from me about what's going on."

The Eagle pulled a chair up next to Alverez's gurney and sat down with his arms hanging over the back. He looked at him for a long time before responding. "Who's in your grave?" the Eagle asked. "My twin brother, that much I will tell you. I had to fake my death to get the feds and cops off my ass." The Eagle stared coldly at Alverez and said, "You're wrong, Mr. Alverez. I will get every bit of information out of you and every thing you know about this plot. You will come to the edge of death many times, perhaps, and think that you will go over,

but I will not allow it. You will tell me everything about this plot and about all those who died at your hands, and you will suffer badly for it. I know all about you and your methods, Mr. Alverez. You were cruel in order to keep your business alive. I'm cruel in extracting justice. I promise you will beg for death long before you will ever taste it."

Alverez laid his head down on the gurney and said no more.

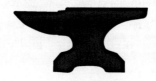

CHAPTER ELEVEN

"Look at him, goddamn you…you have known him for over two decades."

A ndre Espinosa was sitting in a holding cell at the federal courthouse when he heard some chatter about the killing of Patricia Salazar amongst the marshals outside his cell. It had already made the morning news, and he listened as the two marshals spoke, one male, the other female. "So, another in a string of dead cops. That's got to have every department on alert." The female voice said, "From what I understand there is a list, and the list only includes LAPD, no one from any other law enforcement agency." "Someone wants revenge," the male voice said. "If it's revenge that they're after, they appear to also be exposing some very, very bad deeds of these fallen officers." There was a quiet laugh, and the man said, "That's true, Barb. God knows that's true." Espinosa had no sense of time. He only knew that he wanted to get out of there and fast.

A bailiff came down to the cell and called his name. He walked over to the holding cell door, and it opened. Barbara O'Brian stood in front of him and asked him to turn around to be cuffed. "Is this really necessary,

Officer?" "It's the law, Mr. Espinoza. If you don't like it, take it up with your lawyer and a constitutional law scholar." Andre did as instructed and was carted up to the fifth floor and into a courtroom. He looked around but didn't see John anywhere. His court-appointed attorney was asking him questions, and Andre finally asked him to shut up. "This is nothing more than a misunderstanding. Believe me, it's not going any further than this hearing." He heard his name called and stood before the judge. He waved the reading of the charges and entered a plea of not guilty. The judge released him on a small bond of $500, and he paid the clerk and got dressed and out of the courthouse.

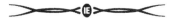

West Valley Police Station was hopping after the news of Patricia Salazar's death. No one was too surprised that she had been killed. It was the way she was killed that had the entire department on lockdown. The orders for lockdown on the offices came from Captain Brian Boyd, and they were deadly serious and to the point.

"There's a killer out there, and he is hunting us. We must be diligent, and we must be fearless in the face of this cowardly enemy who won't show his face but will methodically and meticulously kill sworn police officers." He had sent that out as a memo and read it over the loud speaker to the station. Boyd was hunkered down in his office when one of his subordinates came to him and asked if he was going to take a spin up to the crime scene at Tampa and Vanowen. "Why would I go up there? It's being handled by every law enforcement office in the damn state. My presence there is only going to put more people in close quarters." Lieutenant Riggs McEllen wasn't one to mince words.

"Captain, if you don't go up there people are going to get the impression that you're afraid." Boyd looked at him and said, "I don't give a damn what people think. I'm not going up there because I have not been asked to go up there. I have a department to oversee. If they want me there, they will call me." McEllen walked out of his boss's office and several other

officers were laughing and mocking Boyd. "If they want me there, they will call me!" one of the other desk officers parroted from the reception center of the outbuildings being used while the station was being rebuilt. The desk officer looked at McEllen and asked, "Aren't you friends with Sheriff O'Brian?" He nodded. "Hey…you want to have a laugh? Call the sheriff and ask him to have the captain come up to the scene." McEllen laughed and said, "Okay, but I swear to God if Jim calls Boyd to come up and anyone tells him I got that done I will kick the shit out of you."

There were only two other officers with him, and he was about to make the call when the phone on the main switchboard rang. "West Valley, Lieutenant McEllen." "McEllen? What kind of faggot name is that?" There was a laugh, and Riggs said, "Sheriff O'Brian, you faggot Irish prick. What the fuck do you want?" They both laughed, and then Jim got serious. "Hey, Riggs, I need to speak to Boyd." "Oh, Jim. He's scared out of his skull. If I put you through to him, he will shit his pants." Jim laughed and said, "Then what the fuck are you waiting for? Put me through to that coward." Riggs buzzed Boyd's office, and Boyd jumped at the sound. "WHAT?" "I'm sorry to bother you, sir. I have Sheriff Jim O'Brian on the line asking to speak to you." Boyd cleared his throat and said, "Oh…well…um…I'm in a pretty important meeting right now. Ask the sheriff if I can give him a call back in a day or so." "Yes, sir." The office was busting a gut as Riggs had the conversation on a one-way open line so all could hear.

"Jim, I just spoke to the Captain. He said he is in an important meeting and asked if he could call you in a day or two." Jim yelled at the top of his lungs, "THAT FAGGOT PUSSY PIECE OF SHIT…BY GOD, YOU TELL HIM TO GET ON THE LINE, OR I WILL COME DOWN THERE AND GET HIM MYSELF!" The office fell silent with Jim's comments, and unfortunately for Riggs and the rest of the men, O'Brian was loud enough on the speakerphone that Boyd heard him in his office. Boyd bellowed out his office door, "Did that son of a bitch just call me a coward?" "Yes, sir. I'm sorry, sir," said Riggs. "What the fuck are you sorry for? You didn't say it. Put him through." The call was patched through, and Boyd answered the line.

"Jesus Christ, Jim. Why the fuck did you have to say that to my men?" "BECAUSE IT'S THE FUCKIN' TRUTH! NOW GET YOUR PUSSY ASS DOWN HERE TO PETE'S PLACE NOW!" Jim dropped the line, and Boyd was still holding the phone. He grabbed his coat and hat and walked out of the office saying nothing to the other men. He knew that he had been called out, and he had to deal with Jim head on.

Boyd got to the crime scene a little before noon and saw Jim off in a corner of the parking lot smoking a cigarette and talking to a man in a wheelchair that he didn't recognize and Jade Morgan, who he knew all too well. She, too, had a cigarette in her hand. Boyd got out of the car and walked slowly over to the three. Jim saw him coming and asked, "Where's your fuckin' cigar, asshole?" Boyd approached but didn't answer. Jim said, "I doubt that introductions are in order but just in case, this is Jade Morgan, the autopsy queen, and this is Special Agent Steve Hoffman, FBI." Boyd looked down at Steve and said, "Jesus, Steve. I didn't recognize you. What happened? What put you in a wheelchair? The last time I saw you, you and Molly were having a party at your home."

Jim looked down at the ground, and Jade took a hit off the cigarette and threw it on the ground and said while stamping it out, "You don't keep up on current events, do you Boyd?" She started to walk off in disgust when Steve reached out for her arm, and she put her hand on his shoulder. He looked at her and said, "It's okay." She just shook her head with her hand firmly pressed on Steve's shoulder and said, "No, Steve, no…it's not okay." She shot Boyd a dirty look and walked back into the bar.

Jim wasted no time. "Since you're completely out of touch with the world, dumb ass, Steve's wife passed away of cancer a few years ago, and Steve was recently diagnosed with ALS." Boyd looked away, and Jim grabbed his arm and pulled him back and said, "Look at him, goddamn you…you have known him for over two decades. The man is dying, and he's on this goddamn crime scene and investigating the death of one of your officers. Jesus Christ. I can't believe that you're the president of the police union." Boyd looked at Steve and said, "I'm sorry, Steve. I didn't know." "It's fine, Brian. Look, we asked you

here because your officers are getting slaughtered in chronological order, and I know you know that you are next on the killer's list." He nodded a weak nod. "Are you scared, Brian? Does the thought of a guy blowing your head off or slipping poison into your food or blowing up your car with you in it make you want to piss your pants?" Jim asked. He was in Boyd's face, and it was Steve who pushed back and said, "He has a lot to deal with, Jim. Cut him some slack."

Jim rifled off at Boyd and Steve, "Fuck you, Steve. This guy's a pussy. If he were any kind of peace officer and leader, he would have been one of the first on scene after the explosion. But no, this asshole's hiding behind his desk. Guess what, Brian? It won't save you. The killer is very, very sophisticated, and he will get you unless we can stop him." Brian's face sank, and he looked at Steve with pleading eyes, but Steve nodded in agreement with Jim. "So…what do you want me to do?" Boyd asked looking defeated in his posture and demeanor. Jim looked at him and said, "First, be a damn man, and second, get ready to be bait for the killer. We're going to put you and your family under surveillance and hope that we can lure the killer out." "Use me but keep my family out of it!" "No can do, buddy boy…you're fucked just like the rest of the ones who are dead. We have to go on the assumption that your family is in play here, too, so you're going to have to work with all of it." Jim had just finished the last part of his lecture to Boyd when John pulled up. Steve and Jim looked on as John stepped from the truck stone-faced, his giant frame strolling toward the men with a confidence that told them that he knew something that they didn't…and whatever it was, it was good.

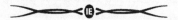

Andre Espinoza was out of jail, but he knew that his problems were far from over. He was now on the FBI's watch list, and there was no way to get that monkey off his back. He pulled his cell phone and made a call.

"Andre, please tell me that you're not calling me to post your bail?" Andre said nothing. "So, the FBI got you. I told you not to fuck around with Swenson. He's dangerous. Now you have his attention as well as the sheriff and Hoffman. So what are you going to do?" "Kill them!" said Espinoza. There was laughter on the other end of the line. "Really? Do you think that that is the prudent course of action given the scope and depth of this mission? Do you think the fact that you're already on their radar is not going to resonate with every law enforcement agency in the city and state? In short, are you really that fuckin' stupid?"

"Swenson humiliated me." There was another laugh. "No, Andre, you humiliated yourself. You also tipped your hand, and I had to use someone else to take out Salazar because you were sitting in jail. Now, there's good and bad in the fact that I did that. It's good because it's going to take attention off of you because you have an airtight alibi. It's bad because I had to use our secret weapon." Andre didn't have to ask who was used; he knew. "So what now, sir?" "You keep to the mission. Forget about Swenson. By the time Swenson and his men know the truth, it will be too late. Then we can turn our attention to eliminating him and the others. Swenson will drop the charges against you today." "How do you know?" "I know. Trust me. He doesn't want you distracted from the mission either. Swenson is banking on catching you in the act. So get in position for the next kill." The line went dead, and Espinoza looked out at Spring Street from the steps of the federal courthouse and on to Olvera Street where the last victim was done in. He walked down the steps and called for a cab to take him home to change.

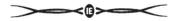

John was talking to Jade and after a few minutes of conversation he walked back over to the two men. Steve looked at John and asked, "So, what do you have?" "I don't have anything. The Eagle does." Jim got close to John and asked, "Yea, whatever. What does the Eagle have?" "Alberto Alverez." Jim and Steve both looked on in

disbelief. Steve said, "Um…I hate to break it to you, but that guy is dead and is a big reason all of this started." John just shook his head, and Jim asked, "What do you know?" "Nothing yet. The Eagle will deal with him." Jim looked on at the burned out wreck of Salazar's car and asked, "Did he do this?" John nodded. "I don't get it. Why would a dead guy come back to life to kill a cop?" John shrugged and walked over to the car.

There was a yellow tarp over the passenger and driver's side windows. He pulled the driver's side tarp back, and Salazar was slumped over the wheel, burned to a crisp. Her mouth was open, and her head was down. If he hadn't known who it was, he could never have discerned from the scene if the victim was male or female. John threw the tarp back down over the car and asked, "Is anyone going to remove the body? We know how she died. This one doesn't need an autopsy to give us a cause of death; I witnessed it." Boyd heard the words come out of John's mouth, but he had no idea how to respond. John looked at Jim and asked while pointing at Boyd, "Who's this?" Jim smiled and said, "Special Agent John Swenson, I'd like to introduce you to the next dead man walking, Captain Brian Boyd."

Boyd looked at John and asked, "You saw Detective Salazar die?" "Yes. We were staking her out." "You were staking her out, and she's dead. You didn't see this coming? You didn't see the killer?" John shook his head. "How the hell do you three plan to protect me and or my family from this killer if you couldn't protect Salazar?" Jim laughed and said, "It was a car bomb, Brian. We don't know anything about it yet — if it was hard-wired or remote detonated. We don't know if the killer was on scene when she died, or if he is a hundred or thousand miles away." There were a few tense moments, and Steve said, "We can't guarantee your safety or the safety of your family, Brian. All we can do is our best to catch this killer before the killer gets you." "That's not very goddamn comforting, Steve," Boyd said with his hands at his side. "It wasn't meant to be. It's the truth." Boyd was looking down at the ground and asked, "So what now?"

Jim said, "Go back to your office, Brian. I will put a deputy on you, and we will put another out at your home." Brian was walking back to his car when John called him back. "I almost forgot to ask, and since you're the only one alive to this point, do you have any idea who wants you dead or why?" Boyd's expression changed dramatically. "Hell no...do you think if I had any idea who wanted me or any of my fellow officers dead I would hold that back?" John looked at him with a look of confusion and then said, "I think that all depends on how deep you are into this situation. I think it is a matter of will you go to prison if you reveal who you think or know is killing your fellow police officers. Perhaps you want to hedge your bet, thinking that we can kill the bad guy before the secret is revealed. Now I'm a federal agent and a well trained one at that. Jim here is a twenty plus year veteran, and Steve has forgotten more about police work than I know. I'm not a gambling man, Captain, and I certainly wouldn't gamble my life or the life of my family on us getting to the killer before the killer gets to you. So, if you do know something about this, and I think you do, you better speak now, or most likely you will end up forever holding your peace. We can protect you a hell of a lot better if we know what and who we are dealing with."

"I told you. If I knew, I would tell you. I don't know anything." Steve looked at Boyd as Jim said, "You're lying. I've known you too many years, but, hey...it's your life and the life of your family, so you head back to your office, and we will do as we have said to protect you." Boyd went to say something but stopped and walked away. Steve looked at Jim and John and said, "He knows way more than he will ever tell. I don't think we can save him." John nodded as did Jim who added, "Fuck him. When he gets killed, it will be his own damn fault." Jim pulled his phone from his hip and took a cigarette from his top left pocket and walked off while ordering deputies to protect Boyd. Steve looked up at John and asked, "Can the Eagle stop this?" John shrugged and said, "I don't know."

Boyd got back in his cruiser and went back to his office. When he pulled into the lot, there was a sheriff's car, and he walked into the front office. Two deputies were waiting for him. They introduced themselves and gave him instructions on how he was to behave while under their protection. Brian invited them back to his office and said, "Well, Jim doesn't waste any time, does he?" Both deputies looked at him and said, "We are part of the sheriff's SWAT team. We are well trained, and we are going to do our best to protect you. You have to do your part by following our instructions." Boyd nodded as they told him what to do.

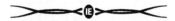

Jim, Steve, and John grabbed Jade and talked to her about Salazar's body. It was pushing eleven a.m. and nothing had been done with it. Steve was asking when she would remove it, and Jade was short with them. "Look, the chick in the car is cooked. I'll do an autopsy on the remains when I get the chance. Right now I have multiple murder victims in this damn bar, and I'm trying to bag and tag them, so I can get them to my office. You three are obsessed with one dead cop. Have you not taken notice that there are at least a half dozen dead men in here?" John nodded and apologized and said, "I know what's in there, Jade, but that scene is not directly related to the case that we are working on. You have to work with LAPD on the bar case while we work on the killer, or killers, of LAPD officers." She just walked back into the bar without saying a word. John called for his CSI team and ordered them to work the car and to take Salazar's body to the coroner's office as soon as they cleared the scene. Steve looked at John and said, "Don't you have some work to do on this case offsite?" John nodded and left the scene.

Jim looked at Steve and said, "I have my best men on Boyd, but I have a feeling he's already a dead man." Steve nodded as Jim asked, "Hey, didn't you two arrest a cop yesterday at the Washington crime scene?" "Fuck, shit," Steve said, "I need to get those charges dismissed and get someone on that fucker." "You think he's dirty?" Jim asked.

"Oh yea…he's in this whole thing up to his fuckin' ears." Steve called one of his agents over and ordered him to take him downtown to the federal courthouse. Jim cleared the scene with his office and headed for Boyd's. He wanted to talk to him some more about what he was certain he knew about this case.

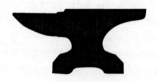

CHAPTER TWELVE

*"Oh shit…every time I
see you hell follows."*

Chris Alton had no idea that Pat was dead until she reached the office at West Valley. She reacted coldly, and her fellow officers didn't understand. One of the female officers that had been with her at Pete's the night before looked at the indifference on Chris's face and asked, "Are you okay? Did you hear what we just told you?" Chris looked at them and said, "I heard what you said. Is there anything I can do to change the fact that she's dead?" The reactions to her response were varied. "She was on the LAPD death list. Did you know that?" Harris Bailey asked her. "No, I didn't know that, but again I can't change it, and I'm not on the list." Chris walked off down the hall to her office. She poured a cup of coffee and sat down in her chair. She leaned back against the chair and felt the sting of Patricia's cigarette burns. She smiled with a sense of pleasure from both the pain of the burns and the fact that Patricia was dead.

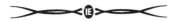

A gas company truck was parked at the corner of Topanga Canyon Boulevard and Viewridge Road near the intersection of Hodler Drive. Dale Hart had received a service order for a home in the eleven hundred block of Hodler and had an order to investigate a possible gas leak at an unknown location on the street. Several residents had reported the odor, and Hart walked the street with some instruments in his hand to detect the gas. He had his head in the air and was sniffing as he walked. A young woman came out of one of the houses and asked if he was there about the gas smell. He told her yes, and she pointed to the middle of the street and told him that the odor was the strongest there. He walked in the direction that she had pointed, and the woman walked back into the house.

She had no sooner made it into the front foyer of the house when the phone rang. She rushed to catch it before it went to voicemail but missed the call. She looked at the caller ID and saw it was her father, Brian Boyd. She took the cordless phone off its stand and walked back out into the backyard where she had been sunbathing. She had a summer wrap around her bikini and dropped it and took off her top and bottoms. She lay nude on a chaise lounge chair and called her father back. "Hi Daddy. I'm sorry I missed your call. I was out talking to the gas man. He's out looking for the source of the gas smell we've had in the neighborhood the past few days. What's up?"

Kristine Boyd had just graduated from high school and had taken a job in the village on Topanga at one of the shops before she started her freshman year at Pepperdine University. She had a bubbly personality and was a bit overweight for her height. She was also well endowed, voluptuous, and athletic. She was laying with the phone to her ear, her long black hair hanging off the chair as not to create a tan line anywhere on her soft, young skin. Her brown eyes were covered by a pair of oversized sunglasses, the kind celebrities wore, and she kicked a leg up in the air, and its muscular flex glistened with suntan lotion.

"Kristine, where are your mother and brother?" Brian asked. "Um…I'm not sure. Mom yelled to me at about nine that she and Alan had some appointments, and that they would be gone most of the day." "Well, I have been trying to get your mother on the phone for an hour, and she's not answering her cell. I called Alan's phone, and he isn't answering either. And you and I know exactly what they're doing." Kristine stretched her tan body on the lounge and said, "Oh, Daddy, don't be gross. I know what you're thinking. They may not be related by blood, but the thought of the two of them getting sweaty together is just disgusting. You've accused Mom of that for years. I don't see it, and I don't keep track of what she does. You know that, and Alan is only out for three weeks to visit. He's your stepson. Didn't you talk to Mom last night? Didn't she tell you what they were doing today?" "No…and I need to talk to them and you." "Okay, well, you have me, Dad. What's up?"

"There are going to be two sheriff's deputies showing up at the house any time." She sat up and asked, "Why on earth would the sheriff be coming here?" "Just listen to me. They are there to watch out for you and your mother and stepbrother. When they get there, do whatever they tell you to do. Understand me?" "Yes, Daddy. I understand." She heard the doorbell while she was still talking. "Daddy, there's someone at the door." "Answer it but keep me on the line with you." Kristine walked through the house and looked through the peep hole and saw two sheriff's deputies standing at the front door. "It's the sheriff." "Well don't just stand there, open the door." "Hold on, Dad. I was sunbathing, and I'm naked."

She grabbed a beach towel off the back of a chair in the dining room and opened the door. The deputies both introduced themselves, and she handed the phone to them at her father's request. She heard parts of the conversation as she looked at the two deputies who were both really, really cute. They handed her back the phone, and Brian told her to listen to what they told her, and he would see her later. She hung up the line, and one deputy stood guard at the front door while the second followed Kristine to the back yard

where she proceeded to drop her towel and walk back to her chair. She said to the deputy who was standing near the gate to the back yard, "It's okay to look and even touch if you like. I'm eighteen." The deputy just shook his head, his mirrored sunglasses covering his eyes. He stood at attention near the gate as she lay down. She put her ear buds in and pressed play on her iPod as a song from Three Doors Down started playing.

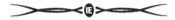

Dale Hart was still trying to trace the odor of gas when he saw the sheriff's car pull up in front of the house. He watched as two deputies got out of the car and then disappeared into the house. He walked back to his truck and grabbed a steel manhole cover hook and walked back to the middle of the street. The steel hook looked a lot like a jack handle, but it was covered in a thick, black rubber, so it wouldn't create sparks when he slammed it into the cover to open the hole in the street. He was just about to climb down the ladder into the tunnel when he saw a man in a gas company uniform standing across the street from him.

Dale waved, and the man waved back. He stood up and walked over between the houses to greet his fellow worker. As he approached, the man walked back behind the house and a large bunch of bushes. Dale called out, "If you're looking for the gas meter, it's on the other side of the house." "Yea…thanks," the man's called out, "are they all on the same side?" Hart approached the bushes while saying, "They are all on the same side on this side of the street and opposite on the other side. Are you here for the leak? Because I was dispatched to deal with that." Those were the last words that Hart would say as a pair of hands reached out and grabbed him, dragging his small frame into the bushes.

There were murmurs and gurgling sounds as blood splattered onto the branches of the bushes. Dale Hart had been disemboweled. His eyes were open in a dead stare as his intestines were squirming on the ground and around his gut. Hart's pupils were still pinpoints, and as they

slowly dilated, his killer looked on at him and said, "It's a bitch, ain't it? Sorry about that, but I have a mission to complete. You have a great death." With that, the killer emerged from the bushes with all of Hart's equipment as well as his ID and the keys to his truck.

He walked across the street to the open manhole and lowered himself down. The hole wasn't a part of the local sewer system. The neighborhood was a newer development, and this was a smaller line set up for utilities, gas, water, electric, cable, and telephone. He pulled the panel for the gas lines open, and the lines were marked by address. He identified Boyd's address and then shut down all of the lines to the other homes. He made a few modifications to the gas feeds and routed them to Boyd's home. The development of homes was new enough that he knew all of the gas appliances were pilotless, and that the houses were all electric except for the kitchen stove, pool heater, and barbeque, so the pressure would simply build in the lines. He wiped the sweat from his brow as he finished and said, "There. That will build up enough pressure in that fucker's house to blow him sky high." He climbed out of the manhole, put the cover back on it, and walked back up the street.

The deputy who was on duty in front of the home saw him walking and waved him down. The killer knew not to run or do anything suspicious. He had a pair of dark sunglass on with the gas company uniform. He also had two Glock nine millimeter handguns in back holsters on his right and left back sides of his untucked shirt. He approached the deputy who was also wearing sunglasses, and they met in the middle of the concrete walk that led to the Boyd home. The deputy had seen the gas company truck when he and his partner pulled in and asked, "Are you reading meters?" "No, no. There was a report of a gas leak out here, and I was sent out to check it out." The deputy was staring at him very carefully. "Did you find a leak?" "Yea. I just had to make a few adjustments and route a line or two. The gas is off to the neighborhood until I can call it in to run a line check for my fixes. The valves are automatic, so, once cleared, we can reopen them remotely. You look like a lawman on guard."

The deputy didn't respond right away, and when he did he ignored the comment. "You look familiar to me. Can I see your ID?" The man handed the deputy his ID, and the deputy took the radio that was clipped to his bulletproof vest and made a call. "Dispatch, I need you to run an ID for me." He gave the information on the ID badge to the dispatcher and waited for verification. The gas man waited impatiently and said, "If I had known you were going to harass me, I would have kept walking." "And I would have shot you," the deputy said while waiting for a response from dispatch. The radio on his vest chattered, and the dispatcher came on and said that the ID checked out as a gas company employee sent out to check for a gas leak. He handed the man back his ID, and as he was turning to leave the dispatcher came over and said, "Unit forty, the gas company advises that they have not heard back from the employee with regard to the leak, and that they have been trying to reach him on his phone and radio, over."

"Why haven't you called in your findings to the company?" "I left my phone in my truck. I was going to call it in when I got back there, man. Shit. I thought I was on a wild goose chase." "But you found and fixed the leak?" He nodded. The deputy looked at the ID and said to the dispatcher, "Mr. Hart has advised me that he left his phone in his truck but that he found and fixed a non-major leak." The deputy pointed at Hart and said, "Is that right?" The killer nodded. "Roger that, unit 40. The dispatcher at the gas company asked Mr. Hart to call in when he gets to his truck, so they can close the service ticket." "Roger. I will advise him." He handed Hart back his ID and said, "You heard what your company wants, right?" "Yea...I got it. I will call when I get back to my truck. Can I fuckin' go now?" "Get the fuck out of here, and next time don't waste an officer's time. Do your damn job and have your equipment on you."

The killer walked back to Hart's truck. The deputy watched as he made a call on the radio and then drove off down Topanga headed into the valley.

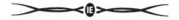

Estrada dumped the gas company truck behind a gas station at the corner of Victory Boulevard and Topanga. It was half past one p.m., and he walked into the station and got a key for the bathroom where he changed into street clothes and walked up Victory to an apartment complex where he had parked his car and headed back to West Valley station. He made one call and said, "Boyd's house is ready for him. Do you want me to try and take him out at the station?" "No...let him go home. Make him feel comfortable. Let it look like an accident." "There are sheriff's deputies at his house. It looks like he has protection." The voice on the other end of the line was direct and straight to the point. "Of course, he has protection. He's next on the list. I will talk to Espinoza and have him make a quick kill on Lieutenant Chilton. That will have them running in circles with their mind off Boyd." "Okay. I will go back to the station. If they are at Boyd's home, then I'm sure they are at the station." "They are. One of my moles told me so. Just go back and encourage Boyd to relax. Maybe have a cookout or something." Estrada hung up the line and headed to his apartment to change again and head into the office.

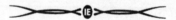

Jim got a call from the OPG garage that Washington's motorcycle had been leased for a month from a bike shop in the valley. He got the address and made a run up to see the owners in the hopes that they might have noticed something before Washington was killed. Jim pulled up in front of the shop, and before he could say a word, Lance Coswalski called out to him from the showroom, "What the fuck does the LA County Sheriff want at my bike shop?"

Jim saw Lance standing in the doorway and sighed and said, "Oh shit...every time I see you hell follows, and I end up getting hurt." Patrick walked out from the back of the shop and Jim said, "Let me

guess? You two own this place?" They nodded, and Jim grabbed the cell phone off his hip and called John.

"Swenson." "I'm standing in front of the mother fuckin' place where Washington leased the bike." "So?" "So…so? Guess which two assholes own the damn shop that he leased it from?" Lance cut Jim off mid-sentence and said, "Rented. We rent bikes. We don't lease them. We sell or rent them." "Oh, go fuck yourself," Jim said. John heard Lance's voice and said, "Jim…Jim." "WHAT…WHAT THE FUCK NOW, JOHN? THE LAST TIME I SAW THESE FACES I GOT FUCKIN' SHOT…WHAT, WHAT, WHAT?" John was calm. "Hand the phone to Lance." Jim drew back and said, "NO FUCKIN' WAY…I TOLD YOU I DON'T WANT TO HANG AROUND WITH YOU ANY MORE, AND I SURE AS HELL DON'T WANT TO HANG AROUND WITH THESE TWO NUT JOBS!" "Hand Lance your phone, please." Jim did as John asked, then walked over and sat down on one of the bikes, took a cigarette out of his top left pocket and said, "I'm FUCKED!"

Lance said, "Hey, John. What's up, brother? Jim is surlier than usual. Did you get him hurt again?" John laughed and said, "No…we are in the middle of a serious situation, and he's stressed out." Lance looked over at Jim who was lighting a second cigarette while sitting on one of the hogs and said, "Yea, he looks stressed. He's on his second smoke. So who did we rent a bike to that's dead?" "A cop."

Lance and Patrick were standing next to each other, and Lance had the phone on speaker and had walked into the empty showroom. Patrick said, "Let me take a guess. Howard Washington?" "Yea…did you two know him?" Lance told him no and explained the situation with Washington and how he came to have their bike. John asked, "When he was at your shop did you see anything out of the ordinary?" Patrick said, "He was a big black fuck with an attitude and was in uniform. He told me that he had a police issue bike of the same model, and that he was looking to buy but wanted to ride the street issue first to make sure he liked it. So, we did a one month rental, and he took off with the bike yesterday afternoon. What happened to him?" "A sniper took his head off in Reseda, and it

was obviously after he got the bike from you guys. Did you see anything, anyone, while he was at your place or when he came in or after he left?"

The two men told John no as their only employee, Gibson Williams, came out of the shop, wiping his hands with a red shop rag. Patrick called him over and asked, "Hey, Gib, you remember that big black cop that was in yesterday and rented the Harley?" "Yup…I sure as fuck do. What an asshole. What about him?" "I have an FBI friend of mine on the line, and he wants to know if you saw anything when the guy was here or after he left." Gib was looking out the showroom window and saw the sheriff's car and Jim sitting in uniform on one of the Harleys. "What's up with the deputy sitting on the bike?"

Lance said, "That's not a deputy. That's the Sheriff of LA County." Gib looked horrified and was backing away when Patrick said, "Gib… don't bolt. He's not here for you. Did you see anything with that cop?" Gib stopped moving backward and said, "Um…not really…I saw him leave the shop with the bike. I remember he was sitting at the light at Ventura. I can't remember if it was on the test drive or after he left the shop with the bike for good, but I saw a cop run across the street and talk to him on the bike."

John asked them to get Jim. Gib stepped back when Jim walked over, and he saw it. "What's his fuckin' problem?" Jim asked, looking straight at Gib. Lance answered, "He's got an outstanding warrant for child support." Jim laughed and said, "Relax, kid. I don't give a shit about that. Why am I here?" John asked Gib to tell Jim about Washington, and Jim asked, "Did you get a look at the cop that ran across the street?" "Um… yea. He was Mexican. He was in uniform and had parked his black and white near the corner." "Did you see any markings on the car? A number or anything?" Gib thought for a second and said, "Yea. He was parked in front of the Belmont Building, the one with the mirror windows. I was able to see the number on the top of the car. It was number fifty five."

Jim took out his midi recorder and had the kid repeat everything then said, "This is really fuckin' important. Are you sure about the number on the top of the car?" Gib laughed. "Listen, dude, there are two things that I never get wrong, the ignition timing when I'm

rebuilding an engine and cops. I'm always looking over my shoulder because if they nab me I'm going to jail for six months even though I have been paying the bitch my current support."

Jim laughed, "How far behind are you?" "Six months." "Yea, it sucks to live in California, doesn't it? The DA can't prosecute and win at criminal trial, but they can beat the shit out of deadbeat dads. How much do you owe?" "With penalties, about a grand." Jim shook his head and looked at Lance and Patrick, "How long has this kid been working for you two fucks?" Patrick told him about a year. Jim said, "Jesus Christ, guys. Loan the kid the grand, and let him get this fuckin' monkey off his back. Then you won't have to worry that he's going to bolt every time a cop comes in. I mean, fuck, is he good at what he does?" Both men nodded. "Then it's a fuckin' no brainer. Give him the money."

They said okay, and Jim said, "No. Give him the money now." Patrick walked off and came back with the cash and handed it to Gib, who smiled, and Jim said, "Come with me." Gib froze. "Relax. I'm the fuckin' sheriff. I have to run the car number to see who was in it, and I will do it down the street at the Van Nuys Sheriff's Station. I assume the warrant is out of that courthouse?" Gib nodded. "I'm gonna make your day. Now follow me." Gib started to walk out with Jim with Lance and Patrick behind them.

John called out on the phone, "Hey, Jim. You want to take your phone with you, or do you want one of these guys to hold it for you?" Jim grabbed the phone from Lance as John told them to come by the house to talk. Jim said, "Oh no...not again, come the fuck on, John. Wherever these two go, my injuries follow." John laughed and told Jim to relax. Jim hung up the line and looked at Lance and Patrick and said, "Why do I have a bad feeling about this?" Patrick laughed and said, "I have no idea, dude. Every time we hang out with you, we have a great time. Right, Cosmo?" "Oh hell yea, C4. I guess we will see you later at John's." Jim walked off, shaking his head, with Gib behind him.

Marco made it into West Valley just before his shift was to start. He walked into the briefing room where Boyd was taking roll call and giving out assignments as well as giving a weak talk about Patricia Salazar's death. Marco saw two sheriff's deputies in uniform at the entrance to the meeting room. He leaned into Riggs who was sitting next to him and asked, "What's up with the sheriff's department?" Riggs laughed and said, "Boyd is next on the kill list. Since Salazar was killed this morning, the sheriff sent protection for him."

Marco shook his head slightly and said, "What a pussy!" Riggs nodded, and Boyd said, "Okay, and finally, as you can see I have a sheriff's detail to protect me, but I don't just want them. I want my two best officers with me as well. Riggs and Marco, you two are assigned to me until the sheriff releases my security detail. I want you two to go to my home and make sure that my family is okay. The deputies will accompany me home later this afternoon." Riggs shook his head, and Marco spoke up and said, "Sir, with all due respect, don't you think that you have plenty of protection? Taking me and Riggs off the street…doesn't that take away from the public's safety?" "My getting killed takes away from the public's safety. Now you two get out of here and get to my house. I don't want you outside. I want you both posted in my home with my family. Am I clear?"

Riggs nodded, and Marco had a look of fear on his face. Riggs saw it and said, "Marco, are you okay, man?" Marco nodded. "Good. I thought you were buying into this whole next in line shit. Come on. Have you ever been to the captain's home or met his family?" He shook his head as they walked out to Riggs' cruiser. "You are going to be very happy you got this detail. His daughter just turned eighteen, and she loves to get laid by cops. His wife is a well-known slut; I mean, rumor has it she's had a thing going with her stepson for a few years. She also likes to fuck cops. She just doesn't let Boyd touch her. His wife and daughter are HOT! Trust me, man. You are going to really, really enjoy this assignment, and I guarantee a stud like you, man, you are going to get so laid." Riggs started the cruiser, and he and Marco headed back to the house that Marco just set up as a death trap.

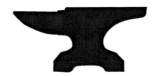

CHAPTER THIRTEEN

The Eagle smiled and said,
"Mercy? No, no mercy."

Jim pulled into police parking at the Van Nuys Sheriff's Station. He got out of his car with Gib, and the two men walked in. All of the deputies and higher-ups saluted as Jim walked in. "Oh, fuck you all. Knock it off. You know I hate that shit!" There was a round of laughter as the men went back to their duties.

Jim handed Gib off to one of his captains and explained the situation. It was just a little after two p.m., and Jim said, "Take him over to the courthouse and clear the warrant. He has the cash. If the clerk or the judge gives you any shit, you tell them I'm handling this personally. And if they still bust your balls, call me, and I will come over. I'm going over to LAPD to run a unit number and see who runs that car."

Jim looked at Gib's nervous face and asked, "The child support warrant is all that's out on you, right son?" Gib nodded. Jim looked at him hard and said, "If there's something else, you better tell me now. If you make me look like a fool, I will throw your ass in jail

and throw away the key." Gib said in a shaky voice, "No, sir, that's it. I just don't have good memories of being here. The judge was really, really mean." Jim grabbed a computer terminal and put Gib's driver's license information into the system. The warrant popped right up, and it was as the kid had said. Jim looked to see who the issuing judge was and shook his head when he saw the name. "Judge Robertson." Gib nodded. "Well, I can see why you're afraid. He's a real hard ass." Jim told the deputy to go back to what he was doing. He would handle this personally.

Jim told Gib to follow him, and they walked next door to the LAPD building. Jim walked up to the front desk duty officer and asked, "I need a trace on this unit and the names of the officers assigned to it." The duty officer took the slip of paper and walked back and handed it to his watch commander.

Jim heard some yelling, and Sergeant Charles Wilson came walking out from the back of the station. "Who the fuck dares walk into my station asking for private police unit personnel?" Charles looked at the front desk and saw Jim standing there with a kid behind him. "Well, ask a stupid fuckin' question. What the fuck are you doing in my police station?"

Gib froze, all one hundred thirty-five pounds of the pimple-faced, six foot, twenty-year-old, bald headed kid. Charlie, as he was known, was a black, bald, nasty cop with a bad attitude and was a well-known racist. "I should have known. If it's not the ginger-faced whitey sheriff of LA County come to harass my police officers." Jim looked at him and said, "Well if it's not a bald headed racist nigger with a bad attitude." "You're one to talk." Charlie pushed the swinging door open to let Jim into the station. Jim told Gib to sit and wait for him. Jim and Charlie walked back to his office, and Charlie pointed to a seat and said, "Sit your white ass down. What the fuck do you want with unit fifty five?" "Don't know yet. It depends on who's driving it." Charlie typed the unit number into his computer and printed off the information.

"So, how the fuck are you, Jimmy?" "Tired, Charlie. Really mother fuckin' tired. You?" "I'd be better if you would find this damn cop killer and get to the bottom of this shit once and for all." Jim laughed and said, "That's why I'm sitting in your chair, asshole. You think I like coming down to the slums of the San Fernando Valley?"

Charlie smiled as he turned and pulled the document off the printer. He looked at it and handed it to Jim. Jim looked at it and smiled. Charlie saw the evil look on Jim's face and asked, "You find who you're lookin' for?" "Do you know Officer Marco Estrada?" Charlie got a thoughtful look on his face and said, "Um…yes and no. I know him from some street work that I did as a watch commander. The guy runs nights if my memory serves me right. I don't know much else about him except he's a spic. They all look the same to me." Jim laughed and said, "We all look the same to you. Jesus! How do they keep a dinosaur like you on the force? Racism is over…at least I thought it was." Jim couldn't keep a straight face as he said it, and Charlie busted out laughing.

"Yea, it's over. We have a spic for a president, so all is right with the world. Fuck, Jimmy, I can't tell the good niggers from the bad anymore. The spics, the chinks, the skinheads, and all the rest of them are just a blend of bad seeds. On that note, who's the kid? He a perp? I need to beat a confession out of someone." Jim laughed again and said, "No…he's a good kid. At least I think he's a good kid. He works for some friends of mine, some ex-military brothers. The kid has a bench warrant on a child support issue. I brought him down to clean it up." "Oh yea? Who issued the warrant?" "Larry Robinson." Charlie let out a howl and a laugh.

"Jesus Christ, and you're going to walk that skinheaded whitey into his courtroom to clear the warrant?" "Yea. He has the money." Charlie got a serious tone and said, "You know that racist mother fucker don't care about the cash. He wants to put everyone in the slammer." "Yea, well, that's what happens when you're the last white judge in Van Nuys. He doesn't care what the race is; he wants to put all of these guys in jail."

Charlie nodded, and both men stood up. "Thanks for this, Charlie. It will help a lot." Charlie said, "All kidding aside, Jimmy, you got to get whoever is killing cops, man. That shit ain't funny. I can't be a racist because I hate everyone. But I do love my brothers in uniform, and I take it personally when one of them falls in the line of duty." Jim looked at Charlie, his face hardened by the war in Vietnam and the war on the streets of Los Angeles, and saw the pain in his eyes. "We will catch him, Charlie." "If you get him, you take care of him, Jimmy. Don't let the media circus start. If you get a beat on him, you take him out. If you can't, then you get the Eagle to do it. I know you know the Eagle, and I'm not going to say anything more about it. I want you to promise me that if you catch the guy that you will deal with him or have the Eagle do it." Jim nodded and walked out of the office. Jim knew what Charlie wanted…the same thing that he did.

In the end, they were all cops, good or bad, and that stood for something. Jim folded the paper and put it in his jacket pocket as he walked out and grabbed Gib and took him to the courthouse to clear the warrant.

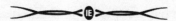

Alverez was groggy when the Eagle walked back into the operating room. The Eagle never spoke. He opened a cabinet and took out some items and placed them in a small orange medical tray, then he walked over to Alverez and took a remote from a nearby table and pressed a button. The table folded in the middle and became a chair. Alberto could feel the cold of the concrete floor on the bottom of his feet, and the Eagle wrapped both of Alberto's legs with two thick leather straps. The Eagle stood up and walked over to the doorway and pulled out a four-by-four cut four feet long and sat down on a stool. He put the piece of wood underneath Alberto's feet. Alberto cried out as sharp splinters drove into them. The Eagle pulled two rusted steel railroad spikes out of the tray and showed them to Alberto without speaking. He then pulled a small sledge hammer off one of the trays next to Alberto's head, and he showed it to him as well. When Alberto saw the hammer, he said, "I'll talk!"

The Eagle never looked up as he held the hammer in one hand and the spike in the other. He just said, "I know you will," as he swung the hammer down onto the spike and through the middle of Alberto's right foot. The man screamed in pain as the Eagle struck it a second time and then did the same to his other foot.

Alberto started to black out, and the Eagle took a syringe from the tray and injected some of its liquid into an IV that was running into Alberto's arm. He left the syringe in and its needle hanging from the IV line. Alberto shot awake, and the pain was twofold. He screamed out for mercy, but the Eagle said, "Where was your mercy? All those kids you hooked on dope? The kids who were running drugs for you? Those mules that you killed as soon as they got the drugs across the border? And now that I want information about the cop killings you ask for mercy? Five police officers have been killed, and there is still a lengthy list of names in your killer's crosshairs. Where is your mercy for them?"

Alberto had tears running down his face and said, "It's not just me that wants these cops dead." "I know that, Alberto, but you know who the leader is." Alberto shook his head. "I don't know who the leader is. I can tell you that. I don't know who it is." The Eagle pulled out a plastic bag and ripped it open. It was a "pedicure kit." He laid the items on a white towel and said, "I don't want you to get an infection." The Eagle pulled out a pair of needle-nose pliers and a pair of vice grips. He took a long hooked item from the kit and drove it under the nail bed of Alberto's big toe and began to rip at the nail to raise it up. Alberto was screaming, and what little movement he could make only made the IV line swing. He started to go out, and the Eagle pushed a little more solution into Alberto's veins, and he came awake again.

The Eagle took the pliers and grabbed the toenail and started to pull and twist it until it released, and he was able to remove the entire nail at the root. Blood, flesh, and tiny thin nerve fibers were left on the surface where the toenail had been. Alberto screamed as the Eagle ripped out one nail after another, never asking any questions, only ripping until all of the toenails on Alberto's right foot had been removed. Alberto was in pain beyond the ability to speak, and the Eagle had all of his cameras on the entire time.

After a few minutes, the Eagle gave Alberto an injection in his right foot, and the pain stopped suddenly. Sweat and saliva were running down Alberto's face, and the Eagle said, "The pain is only gone temporarily. You better start giving me the names of those doing the killing, and you better do it fast…or should I start on your left foot?"

Alberto became quite the chatterbox, and the Eagle recorded the names and information until he had everything that Alberto knew. When Alberto was finished confessing, the Eagle asked, "Who is running the whole show?" "I swear to you, I don't know. I've told you of everyone that I know in this plot." The pain was starting to return to Alberto's right foot, and he begged for more medication. "Half of the names on this list are cops that are already dead. We know of their deeds. Are these two the main killers for this whole operation?" Alberto nodded weakly as the pain intensified. The Eagle gave him another injection, to which Alberto said, "Oh God. Thank you, mercy, thank you." The Eagle smiled and said, "Mercy? No, no mercy. I don't think you've told me everything, Alberto, so let's get started on the left foot, and then I will get to your left and right hands." Alberto let out a scream as the Eagle began to rip out the big toenail on his other foot while pouring salt in the wounds of the right.

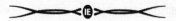

Don Bartell was sitting at his desk at the federal courthouse checking the GPS trackers on his pretrial release personnel. He came to Garrison Cantrell, plugged in his ID number, and the GPS was blinking that Cantrell was at home. He made a note of it and went onto the next subject.

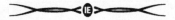

Mark El Compo got word that his next delivery of girls was coming in, and that they were being delivered to one of his safe houses in Woodland Hills. He called Andre Espinoza. "Espinoza." "Andre, it's

Mark. How are you doing this afternoon?" "I've been better. I just got out of jail this morning." "Yea, I heard. Is that having an effect on your police work?" "No…the charges were dropped a little while ago. The agent in charge was busting my balls. I want him dead, but it's been forbidden…at least for now." "Do what he tells you, Andre. You don't want the FBI in this any deeper than they already are. If they get one of you two, this whole thing will fall apart, and we are so close."

"What can I do for you, Mark?" "I have a group of girls being delivered to one of my safe houses. I don't have Washington anymore, thank God. He was killing me by popping all of my cherries. I mean prime grade 'A' meat. Do you have any idea what I get for a virgin?" "Not a clue, Mark. I just get my cut of the action I handle for you." "Well, let's just say at auction here in my main home the really, really fine looking pieces of ass can fetch upward of a hundred thousand or more." "Jesus! Guys will pay that much for some illegal south of the border Mexican pussy? Shit. I have popped plenty of Mexican cherries, and I can tell you it's not worth a dollar." "That's because you're Mexican. These are, for the most part, white men over fifty who want to bust a nut in a virgin…and not just pussy. All of the holes."

There was a moment of silence, and Andre said, "Oh shit. I never thought about getting a total virgin. I can see where that would bring a few bucks, but still, I've done it all with them, and it's boring, other than the screaming. That's fun. I held several down for Howard when he was busting them out. I had no idea that you could have gotten so much at auction. Fuckin' Howard cut into all of our profits." "He did, but you know how Howard was. If we didn't play by his rules, he would have ratted us all out." "So what do you want from me, Mark?"

"I want you to be at the house when the girls come in tonight. You can even bust one if you like, just take an ugly one. There's two that are uglier than a mud fence, but they have really, really hot bodies. There are six really, really hot ones. I need them pure. I will pick them up tomorrow." "What time are they coming in tonight?" "Ten p.m." "Shit. I'm on duty tonight. I will take the time to get the girls in, but I won't be able to babysit them. All I can do is chain them up and leave them for you."

Mark said, "I will send one of my men over to strip, feed, and clean them up. Don't worry about that. If you can just make sure the cargo is safe and secure that will be great. I will have my guy leave one there for you. You can pick her up when you're off shift and do her at the house." "Okay. What do you want me to do with her when I'm finished?" "Oh, shit, I don't know. I don't need her for anything. You want another house servant and sex slave?" Andre sighed and said, "I already have two. I don't want any more. Plus, contrary to what you sell, I had to take a lot of time breaking and beating them into submission." "Well, then fuck her, have some fun, then kill her. Just make sure no one can find the body." "That works. You have a deal." Andre took down the address and information and hung up. He would work his regular shift and take dinner at ten to take in the cargo.

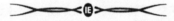

Cosmo and C4 showed up at a little before five p.m. They went to the main entrance and before they could ring the bell, the door opened, and Sara greeted them. She gave them both a hug, and Patrick asked, "Did John tell you we were coming?" She shook her head and said, "Nothing that John or the Eagle does surprises me anymore. And to be honest, I'm glad to see two friendly and capable killing faces." She walked them over to the Eagle's lair and buzzed the Eagle over the intercom. "I know he's here. I heard screaming when I was over here about an hour ago. Relax. I'm sure he will be right out."

Sara had no sooner said it when John appeared through the darkened hallway from the torture rooms. She walked over and kissed him and asked, "Is there anything you need me to do, honey?" John nodded. "I have a guest in room one. I gave him a mani pedi, and I want to make sure his blood loss is minimal. Would you go in and make sure that much pain comes to him?" "But, of course, sweetheart." She excused herself, and John waved to the men to follow him and headed for the conference room.

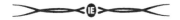

Marco and Riggs arrived at Boyd's home at just past five p.m. They parked their cruiser, and one of the deputies walked up and asked, "Are you our relief?" Riggs shook his head and said, "Captain Boyd asked us to assist with security." Riggs and Marco walked in as the sheriff's deputy remained outside. The house was quiet, and Riggs walked through the foyer and into the entryway to the main house. "Captain Boyd has a hell of a nice home for a cop," said Riggs. Marco nodded, and the two walked into a main room that was split by the kitchen and the family room. There was a double staircase dividing the formal living room, and the whole top of the stairwell was open and led to the second story of the house. Riggs looked around and saw Kristine laying on her stomach in the backyard. He walked out the door, and the second deputy just looked on as Riggs and Marco approached Kristine.

Riggs cleared his throat, and she looked up to see him standing there with Marco and jumped up, fully nude, and hugged him and gave him a deep, long, French kiss. Marco just stared. She pulled away and said, "Jesus, Riggs. You're a sight for sore eyes. I was wondering when my dad was going to send some real cops." She looked at Marco and put her hand on his chest and ran it down from his badge to his crotch and asked, squeezing his package, "Who's this stud?" "Officer Marco Estrada, may I introduce Kristine Boyd, Captain Boyd's youngest daughter." Marco looked on, confused. Riggs saw it and started laughing. "She's legal, Marco. She just turned eighteen a few months ago." Kristine laughed and said, "I am legal, and Riggs made sure he got on and in me at my eighteenth birthday party." "That was a GREAT party," Riggs said, looking around. "So, where are your mom and Alan?" "Um...the last time I saw them she was giving Alan a blow job in the kitchen. They are probably upstairs in the bedroom. I heard her say she wanted him in her ass when I grabbed a drink from the fridge." Riggs kissed her on the cheek and said, "I will do you later!" She smiled while laying back down on the lounge, saying, "You bet my sweet ass, you will!"

Marco followed Riggs into the house and up the stairs until they came to a large door. Riggs said, "Wait here." Marco stopped and stood as Riggs walked into the bedroom. He heard some quiet conversation and a male voice say, "Okay, you can get down on my mom with me but no crossing swords." Marco just stood outside the door while he heard the sounds of laughter and moaning coming from the bedroom. He looked on out to the walkway between the two halves of the house, and as he did he whispered to himself, "I sure as hell hope no one is going to start cooking."

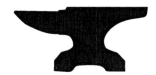

CHAPTER FOURTEEN

"A toast…to the Iron fuckin' Eagle.
He will get to the truth."

J im walked into Judge Larry Robinson's courtroom. He was on the bench, reading some guy the riot act before handing down the stiffest possible penalty allowed under the law. He must have seen Jim from the bench because he made a comment about law enforcement and that the guy needed to learn respect for authority. He slammed down the gavel and adjourned the court for the night. Jim walked up to the clerk and asked to see the judge in chambers.

Larry beat him to it and called out to Jim and his follower, "Come on back, Jim, and bring your little friend with you." They walked back to Robinson's chambers, and Jim explained the situation and sent Gib out to pay the clerk for the warrant before she left for the night. Gib walked back in with a receipt, and Robinson told him to sit. "Since when does Jim O'Brian give a shit about a lowlife skinhead?" "Don't bust his balls. He's a good kid. He works for a couple of my Marine Corps buddies. He's been terrified because he's been paying

his support, and he knew if he came back here you would throw his ass in jail even if he had the bail." Larry nodded, hanging the black robe on the rack next to his desk and sitting down in his chair. "Scare 'em straight or lock them up, Jim. That's my philosophy." Larry looked at Gib sitting on a couch in the back of his chambers and asked, "You ever gonna miss another support payment?" Gib shook his head violently. "See, Jim. Another rehabilitated skinhead. So that's it? You came here to clear a warrant for this kid?"

Jim took a cigarette from his top left pocket, and Larry said, "Give me one of those." Jim handed him a smoke and lit the cigarettes and snapped his Zippo shut. "Well, Larry, that was the only thing I was going to do, but then I got this." Jim handed the piece of paper he had gotten from Charlie to Larry who looked at it, squinting one eye as the smoke from the cigarette rose from his nostrils. "Hmm," Larry said, reading the paper. "These three guys share this cruiser on the daily rotation, huh?" Jim nodded. Larry tapped the cigarette into an ashtray on his desk and pushed it over to Jim. "Don't flick your ashes on my damn floor. You know I hate that." Jim tapped the ashes into the ashtray while Larry put the paper down, still holding it between his fingers.

Jim pulled out his tablet from a holder he had on his chest, pulled up the kill list of officers, and handed it to Larry. He looked at it then looked back at the paper. Larry took another deep drag off the cigarette and stubbed it out in the ashtray and handed the tablet back to Jim. Next, he took a piece of paper and jotted a few things down and handed it to him. Jim looked at what he had written and had a confused look on his face. He finished off the smoke and said, "Who the hell is Mark El Compo?" There was a cough from Gib at the back of the room. Larry took out his own pack of cigarettes and said, "Your young friend back there seems to know the name." Jim turned around, and Gib was standing. Jim didn't say a word. He just turned back to Larry, and Gib made a run for the office door. Larry pressed a button next to his desk, and in a matter of seconds, Gib was back in the office in handcuffs with a black eye. Larry looked at his bailiff and said, "Put him in leg irons. I

don't want him going anywhere." Jim took out another cigarette and lit it, and with his back to Gib asked, "Tell me what you know about Mark El Compo, kid." Silence met his question.

Larry looked at the bailiff standing next to Gib and nodded, and the bailiff hauled off and slugged Gib in the stomach. He doubled over and hit the floor, coughing and gagging. Jim never turned around. He just looked at the printout and the note from Larry and said, "I'm going to ask you again…who is Mark El Compo?" There was a moment of silence, and Larry nodded to his bailiff again, and Gib cried out, "Human trafficking, human trafficking. The guy deals in human trafficking."

Jim took a hit off the smoke while looking at Larry. The sun was starting to set, and the room was getting dark. Larry pulled the chain on a lawyer's lamp that he had on his desk, and the bailiff turned on a double set of recessed lights over the couch where Gib had been sitting, illuminating the floor where he laid. Jim asked, "Is this guy a cop killer?" Gib coughed and said, "I don't know…I have done some work for him. I have helped him get his cargo in from Mexico." Jim didn't look at Gib but asked, "When's the last time you worked for him?" Gib let out a sigh of pain and said, "A couple of weeks ago. I helped him and his mules get some girls and drugs into the valley." "Where did you get them to?" "Um…a house on Vanowen in Reseda."

Jim took a drag off the cigarette and stood up. He looked at Larry and said, "Well, shit, Larry. Ain't this quite the situation? This little fuck isn't just afraid of you. He's afraid of the cops and for a whole other reason." Larry was smoking his cigarette. The room was almost pitch black. The clock on the wall chimed six p.m., and the cherry of Larry's smoke was all that could be seen. Jim said, "Isn't that the clock that Barbara and I got you when you were appointed to the bench?" "Yes, sir. That has been a trustworthy and loyal old clock, Jim. I have had that fucker for near twenty years. How the hell is Barbara doing?" "She's doing really well. I was sorry to hear about Beth. I didn't know she had passed until a couple of days ago. That was another thing I wanted to do, give you my condolences in person."

Jim heard a thud, and Gib coughed. Larry looked on as his bailiff kicked the kid in the chest again. "It's no problem. Beth didn't want her illness and eventual death public. You were on the short list of calls, but I have been dealing with the scum of this city." There was another thud, and Jim turned around to see that Gib was now seated on the couch, bleeding from his nose and mouth, and wheezing. "Sounds like you have some cracked ribs there, Gibson. I know my friends had no idea what you were doing in your spare time, or they would have brought it to my attention or..."

There was a moment of silence, and Larry said, "The Iron Eagle." Jim nodded. Larry sat back in his chair after stubbing out the cigarette and asked, "So, what do you want to do with this guy?" Jim looked at Larry but spoke to Gib, "When is your next pickup for Mr. El Compo?" "Tonight. At the pier in Long Beach." "What time?" "Eight thirty. There's a boat that has been passed through customs. I'm supposed to be there with a cargo van to pick up the merchandise." Jim stubbed out the cigarette in the ashtray and asked, "What's the merchandise?" Gib coughed and said, "If I tell you, they will kill me!" Jim and Larry let out a laugh simultaneously.

Jim stood up and walked through the dark office into the light and lifted his foot to Gib's head and said, "You really should be worrying about me. What do you think I'm going to do to you?" Gib laughed and said, "You're the sheriff of LA County. You can't kill me. You're a cop. So what? You throw me in jail? Fine. At least I will be alive." Jim let out a little laugh and leaned down and peered into Gib's eyes and said, "You're right. You know when you're right you're right. I'm not going to kill you. Neither is Judge Robinson over there or his bailiff who is one of my sheriff's deputies. Nope. You're right. You have no mortal fear from any of us." Jim took a deep breath and called out to Larry, "You mind if I take this piece of shit with me?" "Not at all. I will have the bailiff take him to my private entrance. You can pick him up there."

Jim exited the now vacant building, and Charlie happened to see him running, or attempting to run, toward the parking lot. Charlie walked out the front door of the LAPD office and headed in Jim's direction.

"You know something?" Charlie asked. Jim stopped and looked at him in the halo of a streetlight and nodded. Charlie walked up to the passenger's door of Jim's car and said, "Since skinhead ain't with you, you got something from him." Jim nodded. Charlie popped the passenger door open and asked, "You want some company?" Jim nodded once more, and the two men got in the car. "Do you need to call in to clear yourself?" Jim asked. "I'm off duty, and if you're going where I think you're going, I'm not a cop right now." Charlie took his badge off and laid it in the cup holder. "I don't know what we are walking into Charlie. You could die." Charlie laughed and said, "No one lives forever, Jimmy, no one lives forever."

Jim pulled around to the private entrance of Larry's chambers, popped the trunk of his patrol car, and walked over to Gibson who was barely standing. "You're right about everything, Gib. None of us can hurt you, so I'm taking you to someone who won't hesitate to do what none of us can." The bailiff lifted Gib in his arms and dropped him in Jim's trunk. Gib started looking around when he heard another door on Jim's car open. It was dark, and there was only the light from the streetlights overhead. He heard Larry and Jim talking quietly, and then he heard a familiar voice and knew right away who it was.

Charlie, Larry, and Jim stood in front of the open trunk. Larry's bailiff appeared with a glistening container, and the three men all had sparkling glasses in their hands. Gib heard the sound of glasses clinking, and then he heard Larry say, "A toast...to the Iron fuckin' Eagle. He will get to the truth." Gib started screaming as Jim slammed the trunk shut.

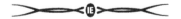

Lieutenant Harry Chilton had just finished up some paperwork and was getting ready to call it a night when his cell phone rang. He answered it and sat listening. He cursed under his breath as the caller spoke. He finally broke his silence and asked, "Where the fuck is he?" He hung up the phone and put it back on his hip. He walked

over to an armory that he had in his office and pulled out an M16 from the case and several magazines for the weapon.

Doyle Markham walked into his office while Harry was checking the weapon out through the armory depot. At six foot, one eighty, with long blond hair and green eyes, Doyle was the pretty boy of West Valley. "Where the fuck are you going with that artillery?" Harry was looking down the sight after clearing the weapon chamber and said, "I just got a tip that our cop killer friend is going to skip Boyd and has his sights on me." Doyle laughed and took the weapon from Harry and put it back in the armory. "You don't want to go walking out the door with a fuckin' M16, man. It's not going to give you the protection you need." Harry looked at him and asked, "Well, just what the hell do you suggest?"

Doyle shook his head and walked into the armory and told Harry to follow. At five foot six and two hundred pounds, Harry was squat heavy with a beer belly. The fact that he was married baffled not only Doyle but everyone in the department. He kept his head shaved and sported a goatee that everyone including his wife thought looked stupid, but he didn't care. Doyle pulled a full set of body armor from the unit and said, "Strip!" Harry looked at him like he had three heads. "You're gay, Doyle. I'm not." Doyle laughed and said, "Strip, you dumb shit. You're not my fuckin' type. Do you want to have half a chance of staying alive?" Harry stripped down to his underwear.

Harry strapped on the shin and calf armor and worked his way up his thigh with Doyle helping him. He put on the vest and arm armor and was about to put on his t-shirt when Doyle handed him another vest. "Shit, man, how the fuck am I supposed to move in all of this?" "You will get used to it. You were arming and getting ready to walk out of here like you got a tip on where the killer will be." "No...I got an anonymous call on my cell saying I'm next on the list. I figure if I'm armed he might think twice."

Doyle laughed and held out his hand and placed his left finger on Harry's right side and said, "Mary was tortured and nailed to a tree. Mario and Washington had their brains blown out by a sniper. Gil was

poisoned, and Patricia had her car blown up with her in it. I really don't think he's going to try a sniper shot on you. Plus, you don't live or work in an area that would be conducive to that. The body armor will deflect most small arms and even slow down a high power bullet." "And if he goes for a head shot on me?" "Well, you can wear a helmet, but I think you would look ridiculous."

Harry finished dressing and asked, "So, what would you carry as a weapon?" "Where are you supposed to go based on the tip?" "Nowhere, really. It was a call from a guy who said he was a friend and wanted me to know I'm next." Doyle looked around and pulled two Glocks from the armory and signed them out with the body armor. He grabbed three extra capacity clips and handed them to Harry. "Okay. This should protect your fat ass from a first shot attempt to allow you to take cover, and then these guns will be more than enough firepower to engage the enemy." The two men walked out of the armory and back to Harry's office. Doyle said, "You will be fine now, so go home and get some rest." Harry put the guns in his shoulder holsters. He had a total of four weapons on him and felt safe and reassured by Doyle's input.

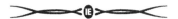

Cosmo and C4 sat down in the conference room with John. He handed them each a document and said, "According to my guest, these two cops are the killers." Cosmo looked at the list and asked, "These two guys are wreaking havoc on the LAPD?" John shook his head and said, "I'm not buying it either. There's someone else, but my source isn't giving him up." Cosmo laughed and said, "Perhaps you haven't leaned on him hard enough." "He doesn't have any finger or toe nails anymore. I removed them." C4 said, "Oh…if he knew anything, he would give it up after that. So, what do you want us to do about it?" "Well, I think we need to grab Mr. Espinosa and Mr. Estrada, and I need to lean on them."

"I don't think that is going to stop the killing." John looked up to see Jim standing in the doorway to the conference room. "What do you know that we don't?" Jim dropped Gib in front of the doorway and said, "Homey, here, has a side job bringing illegals...more directly... Mexican women into the country to be used as sex slaves and indentured servants." Cosmo and C4 looked over to see Gib on the floor, his eyes black, his face beaten. Cosmo said, "I see he fell!" "Yea. For a young guy, he's damn clumsy," Jim laughed as he said it. John looked on and said, "I'll take him from here." Jim said, "He has a pickup at ten in Long Beach. He told us that there are some women and drugs being smuggled in. He's the designated driver." "Told us?" John asked.

"Yea...I had taken him to Judge Robinson's office to clear a bench warrant after I ran an LAPD car number that old Gib gave to me." Jim took the papers out of his pocket and threw them on the table. John looked at Jim and asked, "Did you give Larry my condolences?" "Not directly but having old Gib here, I think, tells you he knows you care about him and his loss." Cosmo looked over at John and asked for the papers. John handed them to him, and he and C4 looked them over. John asked Jim, "So, do we have another name to add to the mix?"

"Mark El Compo." All heads in the room turned to look at Jim. Cosmo asked, "Did you just say Mark El Compo?" Jim nodded. C4 said, "No way...that dude is as clean as a whistle." Jim laughed, taking a cigarette out of his top left pocket. "Yea. A whistle you just blew out your asshole!" Cosmo told John, "Man, we do a lot of business with El Compo. I've been to his home in Bel-Air. There's no way that dude is into this kind of action. We would know." Jim kicked Gib on the floor next to him while putting the cigarette between his teeth and looking at the clock on the wall in the conference room. "Gibson, this might be a good time to start talking, singing, whatever the hell it is you do, because you are in the presence of the Iron Eagle."

Gib looked at the three men in the room and asked, "Which one is he?" "That's for me to know and you to find out. It's ten after eight, Gib. You have a pickup to make. You want to talk to these folks, or do you

want me to turn you over to the Eagle and send immigration in to get the girls and drugs?" "You don't know where to go in Long Beach. You don't know who to talk to. All that will happen if I don't show is the girls will stay on the boat, and their captors will take them back out into the Pacific and feed them to the sharks." John stood up and grabbed Gib by the back of his neck and lifted him until they met eye to eye. "I'm the Iron Eagle. Let me show you what's going to happen to you if you don't start talking." The Eagle walked down the hall, holding Gib like a rag doll. His legs were flopping from side to side as the Eagle disappeared into the darkness.

Cosmo looked at Jim and said, "You're not alone, are you?" Jim shook his head, and C4 asked, "Is the other a good or bad guy?" "Good guy!" "Where is he?" "I dropped him off at Santiago's with a beer and told him to sit tight. It's going to be a long night." Cosmo and C4 nodded and heard Gib's blood curdling scream. Jim sat down across from the other two and said, "I've got a buck that says Gib has become a motor mouth." The two looked at him and both were willing to concede that bet.

John came back ten minutes later and said, "Sara is doing a little patch work on Gibson. He's going to take Cosmo and C4 to Long Beach to pick up the cargo." John looked at the two men and said, "DON'T KILL ANYONE UNLESS YOU HAVE TO!" They both nodded in agreement. "Once you are on the road to the safe house, let me know. I'm on my way to Captain Boyd's home. Gib gave me information that he got a call from Officer Marco Estrada that he is at Boyd's home, and that Espinoza is going to be at the safe house for the girls tonight. I want Espinoza taken alive and brought to me. I'm going to take care of Mr. Estrada."

Sara walked into the room and said, "Your boy is ready." John pointed to Cosmo and C4 and said, "Go get him." The two men walked out and grabbed Gib, and Jim said, "Charlie Wilson is waiting for us at Santiago's." John looked down and shook his head, "You can't get him involved in this. His heart won't hold out. Take him back to the station and tell him the Eagle appreciates his thoughts and desires, but he has it under control."

Jim said, "No…he's tired of this shit, John. He wants it over with, and he is willing to die to end it. Let Charlie, Steve, and I help with this. You have Boyd's killer. Let us follow up on Chilton. He's next on the list." John sat down at the table, and Jim looked at him and asked, "What's going on in that head of yours?" John said, "Garrison Cantrell killed Alberto Alverez, one of the country's most notorious and brutal drug lords and gang leaders, right?" Jim nodded. "Then why do I have Alverez in room one with his feet nailed to a four by four?"

Jim looked on in stunned silence as John said, "The Eagle has pushed Alverez to the brink, and he's not talking about who is running this operation. The Eagle is going to do some dental work on him to try and get more information." Jim asked, "Then who's buried in Alverez's grave?" "He claims his twin brother. There were no dental records to identify the body with because Cantrell blew the guy's head off at point blank range with a shotgun. Jade would not make an error."

Jim called Jade's cell phone. "Morgan." "Hi, Jade, it's Jim. I'm here with John, and we want to ask you some questions about the Alverez murder." "Sure. What do you want to know?" Jim put the phone on speaker, and John said, "Jade, how did you get a positive ID on Alverez with his head blown off?" "Family and friends identified the body on scene as did the shooter, Officer Cantrell. Why?" John asked, "Where are you?" "Sitting in my living room." "Come up to the main house, would you?" "Yea. I'm not dressed. Is that okay?" Jim smiled, and John said, "Yea, it's fine, just wear a robe." The phone went dead, and Jim said, "Oh come on, man. I need some fuel for the fire with Barb." John shook his head and told him to stay put then went to let Sara know Jade was coming.

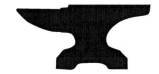

CHAPTER FIFTEEN

*"A toast...to Steve getting his
head blown off before he has
to endure death by ALS!"*

The Port of Long Beach was quiet. The white cargo van being driven by Gibson pulled up to the U.S. Customs' gate. He showed his ID, and the van was passed through. Gibson drove down to the port entrance, and a Customs officer was waiting for him when he arrived near the pier. He got out of the van, and the officer said, "What the fuck happened to you, Gibson?" "I got into a fight." "You were no doubt on the losing end." Gibson nodded, and the agent said, "Follow me." "Do you want me to drive the van down?" "Not yet. My boss has a conference call with Mr. El Compo, and he wants you there." Gibson started to follow the officer, and Cosmo and C4 followed, running through the darkness out of sight of the men. Cosmo and C4 watched as the men walked down to a small Customs building, and they watched Gibson and the agent walk in. Cosmo was on the ground next to C4, and he asked, "Did that Customs guy look familiar to you?" C4 shrugged,

and they moved on down near the water and came up on the backside of the building. They could see Gibson standing off in a corner, and the Customs agent sitting at a desk, but there was no one else around. Cosmo asked, "What does a Customs agent make?" "I don't fuckin' know. He works for the government, so too much for what he does."

Patrick stood up to get a look into the building, and he saw that the agent had a nine millimeter handgun laying on a desk. The agent had his hand over it. "Um...don't look now, but old Gibson is about to get his brains blown out." Lance stood up and saw the gun as well. The two men leaned down, and Cosmo said, "John told us not to kill anyone." "We don't have to kill him. We'll just...wing him." Patrick pulled out his Glock and said, "I will take the front. You cover me. I'm just going to walk in on the meeting." Cosmo smiled and said, "Want to bet that you kill the damn guy?" Patrick nodded and said, "Usual bet?" He nodded, and Patrick headed around the building to the entrance. Lance had not stood back up when he heard a shot. He looked through the window and saw Gibson sliding down the wall; his brains splattered all around him. He watched as Patrick walked into the building, and there were two quick shots, and Lance saw the agent fall to the floor. He headed around the building and ran to the entrance to find Patrick picking up the agent who was looking at both men in terror.

Patrick said, "See, I didn't kill him. I just blew out both his elbows." Lance looked at the officer's name tag and said, "Son of a bitch. I knew I had seen him before. This is Alex Martel. He was the agent in charge of the Eudora Huxley." "Son of a bitch. You're right." Patrick looked at Martel and asked, "Didn't you learn anything from the Eudora Huxley deal? I thought you were an ICE agent?"

Martel looked on. He was in shock. Both from the gun shots and the fact that these two men knew him. "Hey, Martel, I asked you a question. Weren't you an ICE agent?" He nodded slowly. Patrick picked him up and asked, "Where's the cargo?" Martel threw his head toward a small ship anchored in the harbor next to his building.

C4 got over to the ship and took out three guards with tranquilizer darts and tied them up and then herded the women to the van and grabbed the drug cargo.

When they got everything into the van, Patrick went back and got Gibson's body and carried it up to the van. "Well, this is some fucked up shit," Cosmo said. "What?" "Well, the only dude who knows where we are going with this cargo is dead." They checked over Gibson's clothes, and they found a blood-soaked piece of paper with an address on it. "Well, son of a bitch, I think we have a winner. Good old, Gib. He's still helping even from the depths of hell." C4 put the address into the van's navigation system, and it was guiding them to a home on the outskirts of Woodland Hills. It was ten after nine, and Patrick said as they drove up Ocean headed for the 710 Freeway, "You want to let the bet ride? We still have to take Espinosa alive." Cosmo nodded, and the men headed for their destination.

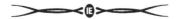

Jim showed back up at Santiago's with Steve at a little past eight. Charlie was sitting at a table drinking a beer when he saw them come in. He saw that Steve was in a wheelchair and asked, "What the fuck happened to you?" Steve wheeled over weakly to the table and said, "ALS happened to me!" Charlie sat silent, and Jim called out to Javier and asked for a bucket of beers. Two buckets with six beers each came over to the table, and Javier walked up behind Steve's wheelchair and pushed him up closer to the table. Javier cracked open a beer and handed it to him. Steve smiled and took the beer and thanked Javier, who smiled slightly and walked back to the bar. Jim said, "The Eagle asked us to follow up on Harry Chilton." Steve said, "Wait. Boyd is next in line." Jim nodded, taking a drink of his beer and said, "The Eagle is taking care of Boyd and his assailant." "Jesus, Jim. You know who the killer is?" "The Eagle knows who two of the killers are, but some things aren't adding up."

Charlie said nothing, only sipped his beer looking off into space. Steve looked at him and said, "Its okay, Charlie. There was no way you could have known." He nodded and took another swig of his beer and said, "Yea...I like it when you white boys get killed off but not like this!" Jim laughed as did Steve, and it even got a little bit of a smile out of Charlie and Jim. "For a nigger who hates whites, I would think you would be dancing a jig!" It was meant as a joke, but Charlie got a serious and sad look on his face. "My father died of ALS. It was one of the worst times in his and my life. He wouldn't use a respirator, so I had to watch him suffocate to death. I hate whitey, but I love my brothers in uniform, Steve. You and me go back a lot of years. I heard about Molly, and I stayed away. I knew I had no right being at her funeral. I suppose that you are not going to be on a ventilator?" Steve shook his head. Charlie raised his beer and said, "A toast...to Steve getting his head blown off before he has to endure death by ALS!" The men cheered, and Jim started talking about where they were going to go to protect Chilton.

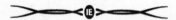

Jade got to the main house, and John and Sara were waiting for her. She was dressed in a sheer robe that hid nothing. John asked her to come in and sit, which she did. Sara asked if she wanted a drink. She nodded. John asked, "When Alverez was killed, he was positively identified?" Sara handed Jade the drink, and she sipped a little and said, "Yea, pretty much. Um...shit, it's been a while. The cop who shot him identified him, and the family was all around as was the media, and they all identified him as well." Did you do an autopsy?" "On what? The cause of death was plain and simple, John. The guy got his head blown off by Cantrell. He was identified, and if my memory serves me correctly, there was no request by LAPD for an autopsy."

John had a bottle of water in his hand, and he took a drink of it and asked, "What if I told you that Alverez is still alive?" Jade laughed and said, "That would be one neat trick because his skull

was in fragments the last time I saw him." John took another drink of his water and said, "Alverez is still alive, Jade." She stopped mid-sip and said, "No way!" Sara nodded as did John. "What the fuck? How do you know?" John said, "Because his corpse blew up a cop car this morning with a cop in it." Jade looked at John and said, "Alverez killed Salazar?" John nodded slowly, looking at her. "How the fuck could you know that, John? I was with you and Steve and Jim on that scene. Jim had that whole yelling match with Boyd, and you were there for it." "I was there before the car blew up this morning. I was there when the car blew up and chased the killer down."

Jade started to get a frightened look on her face, "Then where is Alverez right now?" "He's secure," John said, taking a drink of his water. Jade got a pissed off look on her face and said, "If Alverez is still alive, and you know about it, and he's not sitting in a jail cell somewhere, there's no mother fuckin' way he's secure." "The plot thickens," John said, putting his empty water bottle on the table in front of him. Jade looked at Sara and asked, "Do you know what's going on?" "Only what I've been told, though I have seen Alverez, and he is alive, though he's seen better and less painful days."

Jade shot up out of her chair and ran for the deck off the living room. Sara and John sat still, watching her. She ran for the gate toward the beach and darted off into the darkness. "Should I go get her?" Sara asked. "No... let her spin." "What if she tells someone?" John smiled, stood up, and said, "She won't. The Eagle has to make a house call. When Jade comes back, give her a stiff drink, and I will speak to her when I come back." Sara nodded, and John walked out of the room headed for the Eagle's lair.

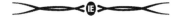

It was ten after ten when the Eagle pulled off the road and parked near Boyd's home. There was a gas company truck parked at the intersection near the house, and there were two men with flashlights checking the street. The Eagle made his way to Boyd's home and saw

the sheriff's deputies standing together outside the front of the house. The Eagle crossed the street and made his way to the back wall of the Boyd home. He climbed over and dropped down into some bushes near the swimming pool. The house was brightly lit, and there was a lot of action going on in what appeared to be the family room off where the pool was. He put an ear bud in his left ear and pulled out an amplifier. He was able to easily eavesdrop on the conversation. He saw an animated young girl yelling at a man who was seated in a chair. The Eagle immediately recognized him. It was Brian Boyd.

The young girl was going on and on, "Why do you get to tell me who I can fuck? I'm eighteen, and I want to fuck your young stud. Alan and Mom have been fucking all day, and Riggs fucked Mom with Alan when he first got here. I want to lay Marco, and there's nothing you can do to stop me." The Eagle looked on, trying to spot Marco Estrada. There were too many people in the room, and he heard Boyd yelling at the girl that he was not going to have his daughter having sex with his officers in his home while they were on duty. He was telling them that they were there for his protection and the protection of the family.

Boyd said, "I'm not happy with fuckin' Riggs right now. Fucking your mother when he's supposed to be out here watching over the family. You and I are going to have words at the station tomorrow, Riggs." "Listen, Captain, your house isn't squeaky clean. Why do you think this psycho wants you dead? So, I fucked Cindy, so did Alan, your damn stepson, so don't give me any shit. It's the only thing that makes me even stay here and protect your ass. If you're that pissed, we will go."

The Eagle saw Riggs point at another LAPD officer who was standing in the kitchen near the stove. Brian said a few more things then asked, "Is this not one fucked up family I have, Officer Estrada?" "It's not my place to say, sir. I'm here at your command to protect you and your family." The Eagle got a good look at Estrada and waited for the next move. He heard the phone ring in the house and heard Boyd yelling at someone on the phone.

"You can't take away my protection!" The Eagle knew it was Jim. His guys had been at the house all day. There was some yelling back and forth, and the phone went flying across the room. The two deputies were speaking into the radios on their vests and walked out of the house. The Eagle heard an engine start, and there was no further sign of them. He worked his way around a dark side of the house on the other side of the family room. He could now hear the conversation in the house without the amplifier. He was hidden under a gazebo and some foliage when he heard the jets of a hot tub start up right above his head, and he moved to the side closest to the house and watched the action through mirrors that were on a wet bar wall in the family room. He could see two women and two police officers, as well as Boyd, and another male. Estrada was hovering really, really close to the stove in the kitchen and that caught the Eagle's attention.

He remembered the gas men from when he pulled up, and he called the gas company and got their automated system and plugged in Boyd's address. The system came back that there was a gas leak of unknown origin and that the company was working on it. The Eagle looked around and saw the gas meter on the other side of the gazebo next to the house. It was shrouded in darkness, and he used a pin light to look at the gauges on the meter, and they were all maxed out. The Eagle moved back over to the edge of the gazebo and heard Boyd yelling at his family members to get ready to go out to dinner. Estrada remained near the stove the whole time, and Boyd came into the kitchen and said, "You are all I have to protect my home, Marco. I am taking Riggs with us to keep guard. The house is your responsibility. We will be out for a few hours. I will have you relieved as soon as we get back." The Eagle heard Estrada say, yes sir, and in a matter of minutes the house was empty except for Marco.

The Eagle made his way to the open sliding glass doors. He saw Estrada make his way to the front door and peek out the glass. The Eagle slipped into the house and into the kitchen. Estrada took out his phone and made a call. "Sir, this is Estrada. I have set everything in motion here. Requesting permission to leave these premises?"

There were a few moments of silence, and Estrada said, "With all due respect, sir, I have done my job. This house is a bomb, and I don't want to get my ass blown to the moon with Boyd or his family."

The Eagle opened all five burners on the stove, and the gas rushed out in a loud hiss. Estrada walked back into the kitchen with the phone still to his ear. The Eagle had made his way back to the corner of the backyard, and he watched the look on Estrada's face when he realized that the valves were open. Estrada looked around to see who else might be in the house with him. The Eagle stood up in a far corner of the yard behind a rock waterfall that made its way down into the pool. Estrada looked over to see the blue steel glint of a weapon, the phone still to his ear.

The explosion rocked the neighborhood; the house had nothing to burn. A gas line burned a hundred feet into the air. Boyd's home had been reduced to tooth picks. The concussion from the blast blew out windows and set off car alarms for blocks. The Eagle walked to the side gate and out into the darkness back to his truck. He knew that Marco Estrada had been vaporized, and he also knew that there was someone in deeper cover running this show.

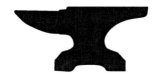

CHAPTER SIXTEEN

*Harry kept running. The second
shot hit him in the right rear thigh,
but the body armor worked.*

The arrow on the GPS was blinking in front of the house on Willins Avenue in Woodland Hills. The van was parked two houses down. There were no lights on in the property, and Patrick got out of the van and made his way up to the house and then to the backyard. The house was empty, and he picked the lock on the back door and walked in. He cleared the residence then called Lance.

Lance pulled the van into the long driveway that circled around the house to the back. He got out and walked in and called out to Patrick who did not respond. "C4, where you at?" "I'm upstairs. Get up here." Lance ran up the stairs in the dark and when he hit the top he stopped dead in his tracks.

Patrick was holding a skull in his hands. There were five empty rooms with steel rails bolted to the floor, with chains and hand cuffs spread two feet apart. Leg irons were bolted to the floor with extra heavy chain. There

were two wooden tables and a queen bed in the corner of the room. The mattress was stained with what the two men could only figure was blood, and every room in the house was set up exactly the same.

Patrick said, "Jesus Christ, man. This is a holding and torture room." Lance said, "No…these are slave's quarters. They chain them in here until they are ready for sale." He pointed to the tables and said, "Those are branding stations. You did notice that every room has a fireplace." Patrick nodded. "They use it to brand the slaves before they are moved for auction." Patrick asked what the other table and bed were for. "The other table is the same, and the bed is where they break the girls in." "You think this is a brothel?" Patrick asked. Lance shook his head. "No. These are training and punishment facilities. Here the undesirables are raped and beaten until they submit to the will of their oppressors. Once they have been broken, the less attractive of this guy's slaves are sold into captivity, either as household servants or sex slaves, most likely both."

A pair of headlights pulled into the drive as the two men spoke, and they made their way down the stairs to see a police cruiser in the driveway. Lance and Patrick walked out, and Andre Espinoza approached. "Where's the kid…Gibson?" asked Espinoza. Lance said, "He's out with a raging headache. We've been sent to deliver the goods." Andre walked to the back of the van and said, "Well, let's see the cargo. I don't have all fuckin' night." Patrick opened the door while Lance stayed behind Andre.

Espinoza took out his Maglite and looked in at the girls. They were all nude, and several were really, really beautiful. "Well, I see why Mark didn't want me to touch some of them. Not only virgin pussy but really, really hot looking pussy. Damn…I really want to fuck a couple of these…I never got to pop cherries like these in Mexico."

Patrick asked, "So, you're a cherry popper?" "Oh yea!…I really prefer the young girls between five and twelve. They are so much tighter and scream a lot more when you rip them than the late teens like these. But these are some really beautiful teens. I'm going to give Mark a call after we unload them and get them chained down to see if I can buy one now and pop her." Lance was standing behind him, and Patrick could

see that he was seething with anger. Patrick said, "Well, why don't you give Mark a call before we take them out. Hell, man, shoot some photos and pick the ones you want us to leave in the van for you."

Andre said, "Great idea. Mark's at my fuckin' mercy anyway. I can fuck any of them I want. I will send him the photos of the ones I'm going to fuck and tell him he can fuck off. Fuckin' Howard used to pop all of the girls as they came in. I can certainly have a few." Andre pulled out his phone and took several shots. The flash on his phone made several of the girls wince and cower. He emailed the pics over to Mark then got him on speakerphone.

"Hey, Mark, it's Andre. I sent you over some pics of the pussy you hauled in. You weren't kidding, man. These are some fine pieces of ass. I don't know which ones you thought were ugly, but there isn't one in the bunch if you ask me. Listen, I know you want all of these girls kept as virgins, but I just can't let go of it. I'm gonna pop a few of them, man. Washington had the best of all worlds. You can afford for me to have a couple of nice pieces of ass."

Mark said, "Come on, Andre. You gave me your word. These are fine grade A pieces of ass and all perfect fuckin' virgin pussy. I already have several bidders lined up, and two that want to buy three of the girls just based on pics alone. Don't do this to me. I will make you a deal. You chain them up like we agreed. I will get a couple of my boys over there to strip, feed, and brand them, and I will give you a thirty percent cut on the sale...what do you say?"

"Money speaks louder than pussy. If you can get what you say you can for them, then I will cut you a break. I will help your guys unload and chain them up." "Guys...what guys? Gibson should be making the delivery." "No. These two guys said that Gibson had a skull crushing headache, and...that...they..." Andre's face started to drop as he realized that he was in deep shit.

Patrick pulled the doors to the van fully open, and Gibson's body fell forward with half his skull blown off. "I told you he had a skull crushing headache!" said Lance as Patrick hit Andre with a

tranquilizer dart, dropping him to the ground. His phone was still locked in his hand, and Mark was screaming Andre's name. Lance answered and said, "I'm afraid that Andre is out right now, but don't YOU WORRY…I'M SURE HE WILL BE SEEING YOU REAL SOON!" The line went dead, and Mark started screaming and running through the house in a panic.

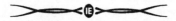

Harry Chilton parked his car in front of his home. This was one of those moments when he was sorry that he and his wife Peggy had purchased a large piece of horse property with nothing but eucalyptus trees and honey blossom bushes around it. From the driver's side door to the entrance to his home, it was a hundred yards, and that included three horse pastures he had to make his way through and a riding ring that Peggy used for horse training and running her horse business. He tugged on his body armor and grabbed for his briefcase and helmet that he had kept in the car for security. He opened the car door and tried to talk himself down. "Relax. You're home. Peggy is waiting with dinner and a drink. The servants will give you head while dinner is being prepared, and you and Peggy can talk about your day." He closed the car door and hit the key fob locking it. He started to walk across the field all the while talking to himself.

The crosshairs on the rifle had Harry's head in the middle. The shooter was kneeling on an old hunter's tree stand fifty yards away. "It's just too easy," he whispered to himself as he led Harry through the grass with the sniper rifle as he walked toward his house. "I need to make this more sporting," the shooter said as he pulled back on the bolt action thirty aught six rifle. He let out a low guttural call, neither animal nor human, and watched as Harry moved into his rifle's sight.

Harry heard the sound as he was halfway across the field. He stopped for a fraction of an instant and looked behind him. A sliver of red light broke through the trees, and he looked at it with a moment of confusion

before he realized he was looking into the laser sight of his killer. He began to run, zig zagging and screaming to Peggy to open the front door. The first shot rang out, and he heard it, and a tuft of dirt and grass arose near his feet. He kept the zig zag movements going as he ran for the house. The front door opened, and his wife Peggy stood in a half open robe, nude underneath. She had a smile on her face and a drink in her hand. Two Mexican servants were on their knees, nude, beckoning to him in Spanish, their young breasts waving with their arms in the air.

The world was moving in slow motion for Harry. He could see the warm light of the house and Peggy smiling and the two young girls calling to their master. Peggy had stepped forward, and one of the girls was on her robe. She drew back and backhanded the young girl on her left, yelling at her to obey her master's orders and not to be under her feet.

Harry kept running. The second shot hit him in the right rear thigh, but the body armor worked. He was still standing and running. He saw the girls getting up as Peggy smiled once again and waited for his arrival. "Enough," the shooter whispered and pulled the trigger. The bullet passed through Harry's skull and right into Peggy's as she waited at the door.

There was a momentary lapse for both of them. Harry's eyes caught Peggy's as he fell to the ground near Peggy and the two girls. Peggy's head jerked back at the strike of the bullet. A fine spray of blood sprung from the back of her skull. She dropped to her knees as if greeting Harry then fell face first onto the ground on top of his body.

The two young girls began screaming and ran into the house. The shooter sat on his perch watching the house for at least ten minutes as the first police car showed up on scene. The shooter packed up his rifle and climbed down from the tree and moved through the darkness and disappeared.

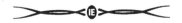

The Eagle received the call from the men that they were incoming with both heavy cargo and a surprise. The Eagle had made his way to Mark El Compo's home in the hills of Bel-Air. He knew that if there was an answer to what was happening El Campo had it. The problem was that Patrick and Lance had made a mess of things. Mark knew that someone was on to him. It was now a race against time for the Eagle to grab El Compo before he got away into the night, perhaps never to be found again.

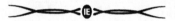

Don Bartell was out making routine probation checks. Tonight was about low risk offenders. He liked these types of checks because he had never had to pull his service weapon on this group. Don was no stranger to the mean side of probation and parole. He had had his fair share of run-ins with the really, really bad guys, and he had the wounds to prove it. He had just finished up with a pedophile that was on house arrest as part of his probation and was happy to find him at home where he was supposed to be.

For the people he had on pretrial release and on GPS trackers without those types of restrictions, home visits were hit and miss, though he always ran GPS tracking on them before he left the office. He could not call to tell them he was coming, but it was his job, and he enjoyed doing it. He arrived at Garrison Cantrell's home at just after eight p.m. He parked in front of the small bungalow and pulled his GPS tracker and plugged in Cantrell's information. The unit showed that Cantrell was in the house.

He walked up to the front door and rang the bell and waited, but there was no answer. He knocked on the door again, and this time he announced himself, "Mr. Cantrell, this is Officer Bartell with the Los Angeles Department of Probation. I've stopped by for a visit." There was no response. He looked back down at the handheld GPS tracker and the red blip of Cantrell's ankle bracelet blinked clearly. He panned out on the unit to see the full layout of the house's interior, and according to his unit, the GPS tracker was only ten feet from the front door. He pounded on the door and called out to Cantrell.

Being a probation officer, and given the fact that Cantrell was under his supervision, the terms of his release allowed forced entry into Cantrell's home. He called out again and said, "Mr. Cantrell, if you don't open the door, I have a right to enter. I have a key to your premises." There was no response. Don put the key into the deadbolt on the house and turned it, but the deadbolt wasn't locked. He tried the door knob, and it was locked. He put the key into the cylinder and unlocked the door and pulled his service revolver as he slowly opened the door. He walked into the small foyer of the house, and there were lights on, and he could hear what sounded like a radio in the distance. There was a doorway directly to his right, and there was light coming from the room and its open door. He walked into the light, but he wasn't prepared for what he found.

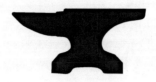

CHAPTER SEVENTEEN

"You really should be more polite
to the wife of the Iron Eagle."

S teve, Jim, and Charlie were finishing their beers when a call came over Jim's radio that there had been a homicide in Tarzana. Charlie looked over at Steve and Jim and said, "I have five bucks that says that homicide is none other than Harry Chilton." The two men looked on, and Jim said, "How the fuck would you guess that?" Charlie held a finger to his lips as the chatter went back and forth on the radio. An address was barked out, and Charlie smiled and said, "Because that's Harry's home address." Jim looked at Charlie and said, "Now, how the fuck do you know that? I know that you and Harry aren't friends." "No, sir, we are not, but I fucked his wife Peggy twice a week for the last ten years. She liked my big black cock in her tight white pussy…and other places!"

Jim frowned and looked at Steve and said, "Are you buying this?" Steve shrugged his shoulders and said, "I don't know Charlie very well, so I have no reason to think he would lie." Jim let out a loud

laugh and said, "If there's one thing I know about this racist mother fucker is he doesn't know how to tell the truth."

Charlie finished off his beer and slammed the bottle down on the table and said, "Oh, go fuck yourself, ginger boy...I fucked Barbara, too!" Jim shot up out of his chair and leaned in to belt Charlie in the mouth when Charlie broke out laughing. He put his hands up in self defense and said, "I'm kidding, you fuckin' mackerel snapper. I would never stick my dick in an Irish chick."

Jim sat back down, and Charlie looked at him sheepishly and said, "Besides, the woman scares the living shit out of me." Jim said, "She should, you dumb ass nigger. Barbara would chew you up and spit you out, and I do mean that literally." That got Steve laughing, and he said through tears of laughter, "Are we going to Chilton's crime scene, or are we going to sit here?" Jim piped up and said, "Why bother? The guy's dead...check another off the list."

Jim was chuckling when they heard about an explosion off Topanga Canyon Boulevard on Hodler Drive. Jim looked at the men and said, "That's an address that I know. I had two of my deputies there today. That's Captain Brian Boyd's home, and I also know that Boyd is alive and well. My men told me he was getting his family out of the house for dinner."

Steve looked on and said, "The Iron Eagle?" Jim nodded, and Charlie just looked on and asked, "Who the fuck's next on the killer's hit list?" Jim pulled out his tablet and said, "Ricardo Pina." Charlie laughed and said, "If Pina's on the list, then so must be Vince Espeno." Jim nodded. "How the fuck do you know that? Did you get a copy of the list?"

Charlie shook his head, laughing. "They have a house in the hills overlooking Sherman Oaks." Jim asked, "Are they out of your division?" "Naw...those fags are out of West Valley. I had the misfortune of crossing paths with them about a year ago when I was in civilian clothing. I picked up a call and a publicity nightmare for LAPD. Pina, or penis as I call him, is the head of PR for the LAPD, and Espeno is the deputy chief of police. Those spic ass fuckers took me for some poor old nigger off the streets. They blindsided me by telling the media that I was a witness in a police

brutality case and would testify that the cops were in the right. The fuckers did it on national television not knowing I was a cop, and when that story broke, they bashed the shit out of me in the media, making up shit, said I misrepresented myself to them, and that I lied about a bunch of shit. Those two fuckers almost got me thrown off the force. I was under investigation by internal affairs, and I would have gotten railroaded off the force if it hadn't been for Garrison Cantrell and the Alverez killing. That took the limelight off me, and my lawyers got the case dismissed.

"Garrison got kicked off the force, and to be honest, for a white boy, Garrison Cantrell was a good cop. The fucker was an honest cop. I will never figure out how they were able to railroad him the way they did. Then to blame him for Mary Schultz's murder. Fuck, man…there was a line of people who wanted to see that bitch dead, including the chick she was fuckin.'" Jim and Steve both looked at Charlie and asked, "Salazar and Schultz were lovers?" "Oh, fuck yea, man. I have it on good authority that they were into some pretty twisted shit…they were two fucked up chicks. Schultz was a kike, man…a fuckin Jew girl munchin' on spic pussy…sick shit, man, sick mother fuckin' shit."

Jim put the beer he was drinking down and asked, "How do you know where Pina and Espeno live?" Charlie laughed, finishing off his beer, "I was going to send a couple of my home boys up and have them kick the shit out of them after the whole mess was done, but I decided to let it slide."

Jim stood up and got behind Steve's wheelchair and said, "Well, you might just get your wish after all. We need to get to their house NOW! We may be the only thing standing between those two and death." Charlie stood up and said, "Oh come on, man…let me at least take satisfaction in those two getting what's coming to them." Jim laughed and said, "It's not just about them getting what's coming to them. It's about getting this nut job cop killer. If we don't, sooner or later that list is going to run out, and I can tell you that this killer has a taste for this now. He's really, really good, and he will turn his sights on others in law enforcement, and that could just as easily be you or me." The look on Charlie's face said it all. The three men headed for the door and Ricardo and Vince's home.

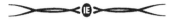

The Eagle made his way up Mark El Compo's half mile driveway. He had two bags on his shoulders, and he was moving through the darkness as best he could. El Compo's home was built on the side of a cliff overlooking Los Angeles and Santa Monica. When the Eagle crested the top of the hill off the west-facing cliff, he could see all the way to the sea. There was a full moon reflecting off the water in the distance, and it would have been a beautiful view if he didn't have work to do. He stowed the bags in some brush beneath the house.

The house was literally built on stilts to take advantage of the view and the hillside. The Eagle heard music coming from the main level, and there were people out on a large patio off the front of the house. He pulled a pair of field glasses from his bag and looked up to see what appeared to be a very, very, formal party going on. Once he saw the number of guests on the double balcony to the home, he knew that there was no way that El Compo was going to bail on his own event. The Eagle pulled his tablet out of his case and typed in the address and Mark El Compo's name into the NCIC. El Compo had an impressive rap sheet, but he had never been convicted of any of the things he had been charged with.

The list of charges were all serious offenses. The sheet read like a who's who in the bad ass world of pornography and pedophilia. The guy had been charged with seemingly everything: false imprisonment; drug, gun, and human trafficking; international slavery and sex trafficking, as well as prostitution. The Eagle read over the sheet then pulled a blueprint of the home from the assessor's office and studied it carefully. He looked at Mark's photograph. He was a good looking guy, six five, two twenty, black hair, and brown eyes.

Mark's driver's license photo looked like an actor's headshot. The Eagle burned the image of Mark into his mind then loaded up with one small bag of gear and headed up the side of the hill just below the lower deck. When he reached the lower level to the home, he pushed himself against a garage door and pressed the button on his remote sensors.

They picked up heavy security. The door he was leaning against had no handle or locking mechanism that the Eagle could see.

He placed a magnetic finder on the door but got no reading. The Eagle used a receiver in his pack to pick up a strong wireless signal that was heavily encrypted. "Digital door locks. Impressive," the Eagle whispered to himself as he pulled out his tablet and began to run an encryption decoding program that sliced through the house's electronic system. Within five minutes, the Eagle had full access to the house. He scanned for all common electronic lock configurations, and he heard the click of a release as his weight against the lower buildup door to the house pushed it open.

The Eagle locked all signals and transferred the lock codes to a flash drive in his pocket. He took out his PDA and plugged the flash drive into it, and in seconds he had his very own key to the El Compo mansion. He took the small bag with him and moved into the buildup. It was pitch black, and he felt for his night vision glasses and put them on. He clicked the switch and could see that he was sitting on a steep hillside under the home. There were concrete pillars with huge steel girders running down into them. The Eagle moved to the top of the buildup and found a concrete walkway that led to another door. He pressed his amplifier against the steel door but heard nothing.

The Eagle pressed a code, and the door lock released, and he pushed it open, and it flooded with light. He removed the night vision goggles and moved into what he realized was the laundry room. There were several industrial washing machines and dryers. There were laundry baskets full of linens. He looked in one that had clean linen in it and another that had soiled fowl smelling garments. The Eagle moved some with his gloved hand and saw feces and blood. He exited the room knowing he now had a point of reference that he could use with the blueprint in his mind; he knew where he was in the house.

When he pressed the 'enter' key on his PDA, the lock released, and he moved out into a well lit hallway. There was a long steep stairwell in front of him and a door next to him. He pressed the enter key again,

and the door unlocked. He slowly pushed it open and saw dozens of nude young Mexican women and girls, gagged and chained to steel bars on the floor of the room. He moved quietly amongst them, and their eyes were huge and full of fear as he slowly took a head count. He took out his PDA and typed a message and hit send.

He moved to the end of the room and put his hand on one girl's shoulder. She cringed, and he put his fingers to his lips, and in his deep natural voice said in Spanish, "You have nothing to fear from me. Keep silent." The room was very, very hot. Down in the middle of the room was the source of the heat...a large domed fire pit that vented up into the ceiling. It had a raging fire burning in it, and there were multiple steel branding irons in the flames.

The Eagle moved over to get a close look. There were five girls all chained face down and arms and legs spread eagle. The smell of charred flesh struck his nostrils, and he could see that the women had each been recently branded. Three had the initials, M.E.C., branded into their buttocks. Two other younger girls had brands that consisted of a circle and two cherries. The Eagle moved back up to the door where the young girl he spoke to sat, and he pressed his PDA and moved through the door and into a mirrored room with one-way glass all around it, and a center stage that was turning.

The Eagle spoke under his breath, "The auction room." The room was darker than the other, and he found his way to another door and pressed his PDA, and the door unlocked and led him out into a hallway. There were voices in the distance, echoing off the walls. "Listen...I want this auction finished up, and I want it done now. Do you understand me? I have a plane to catch, and I don't want my guests to be none the wiser that I'm leaving."

A female voice responded. "I understand, Mr. El Compo, but the girls are not dressed. They're not ready to present to your clientele." "Are they clean?" "Yes, sir." "Then I will go upstairs and announce that I'm going to do a special auction tonight. Instead of covering the merchandise in clothing and trinkets, I am leveling the auction

field. Everyone will get to inspect the merchandise fully nude before bidding." "Okay, sir, but there are five girls in holding. Three of them have just been branded. I branded two more virgins, but there are at least six that I still need to brand."

The Eagle heard Mark El Compo getting agitated. "Brand the bitches after the damn sale. The buyers don't care. Shit. One of the complaints I have been getting is that they want to brand them themselves, and they don't like that I scar their treasures. Just get them ready, and I will take care of the rest of this." There was a moment of silence and then a "yes, sir." The Eagle heard soft footsteps coming his direction and moved back to the holding room and down to the lower door.

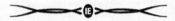

Patrick's phone buzzed with an email from the Eagle. He read it, and a huge smile broke out across his face. He looked at Lance and said, "We need to pack our shit. The Eagle has instructions for us to blow a building in Bel-Air." Lance looked on and said, "What does he need?" "He wants us to bring the van as there will be cargo…I'm betting human. And he wants me to bring enough C4 to level a…" He looked at the email again, and the dimensions the Eagle sent. "A shit load of C4, Cosmo, a fuckin' shit load. Grab my bags. We have to go to the shop on the way out there."

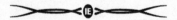

Sara was tending to the girls that had been in the van. C4 called out to her, and she walked out into the foyer. "We just got orders from the Eagle. We have to do some demolition work. Can you handle this?" Sara looked on and picked up a phone on an end table near the foyer entrance, pressed the conference button, and in a matter of seconds she had Barbara, Gail, and Jade on the line. "Are you ladies free tonight?" All of the responses were yes. "I need your help at the main house ASAP. Meet me at the main entrance, and I will explain there." She hung up the line and said, "We

have this. Go do what the Eagle wants." Lance and Patrick ran out of the building to the van. Sara said something to the girls in the room in Spanish and closed the door. She walked down to the second operating room where Lance and Patrick had placed Andre Espinoza. He had been tied down with leather straps, but he was alert. Sara walked in, and Espinoza started cursing at her and struggling against the restraints.

"You fuckin' cunt. You release me this second, or I swear, when I get off this table, I will fuck you ten ways from Sunday, and then I will strangle you with your own intestines." Sara walked over and pulled an IV bag from a refrigerator in the room while Espinoza continued to threaten her. She fixed the IV tubing and put an extra large needle on the end then dropped the uncapped needle and the tubing on the floor while carrying it over to Andre on the table. The veins in his arms were pulsing on the surface of his skin.

"You have made it so much easier to set a line, sir." She stepped on the needle on the floor with her shoe then picked it up and jammed the four inch spike into his throbbing vein. She took a syringe and pulled back to make sure she had a good line, and thick red blood filled the syringe. She taped it off and then walked back over to a cabinet across from the table and pulled out a syringe full of clear liquid. She walked back over to Espinoza and said as she stuck the needle into the IV, "You don't know where you are, do you?" He screamed more obscenities at her, and she said, "You really should be more polite to the wife of the Iron Eagle."

Andre fell silent, and his eyes got as big as saucers as she smiled at him and pushed the solution into his body quicker. He was starting to pass out from the drug when she said, "When I tell the Eagle the things you said to me, well…I don't know the extent of the things you have done that brought you into his lair, but I can promise you it will add tenfold to whatever he is going to do to you." Andre started to make a sound like a scream, but it never made it to the top of his throat. He was out on the gurney, and Sara said to him as she walked out, shutting the operating room door behind her, "You are going to have a really, really bad night as are some other people I fear."

She walked over to the main entrance, and the girls were there. Sara knew that the Eagle's identity was safe with Barbara and would be safe with Gail. It was Jade that was the wild card, but she needed her medical expertise to help treat the girls and get the other rooms ready for what she knew was going to be a long and bloody night.

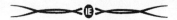

Don Bartell stood in front of a bank of computers. Garrison Cantrell was nowhere in sight. He looked at the screens, and they had all kinds of data flying back and forth on six different monitors. He held up the GPS tracker he had for Garrison, and the signal ended right there. Garrison's unit was sitting on a stool in front of the computers fully intact. It had not been tampered with. It had simply been removed with the proper tool. Don looked around the house, but there was no sign of Garrison. He pulled his phone from his pocket and went to dial when he heard Cantrell's voice behind him.

"I'm afraid that's a call that I can't allow you to make, Mr. Bartell." Bartell turned slowly to see Cantrell in camouflage clothing and face paint standing in the doorway behind him. "It's been you all along…you're the one killing the police." Cantrell was holding a nine millimeter with a silencer on the barrel.

"Pretty damn brilliant, don't you think? I mean, I have to be honest, when they released me on pretrial release and then with the GPS, I was a little worried. But then they assigned me to YOU… Mr. Nice Guy, also Mr. Lazy Guy. I knew that the odds that you and I would cross paths outside of your office were slim to none. I also knew that I ran a risk of you making a house call and me not being here and that could be trouble. Such a wonderful confluence of events. My team has finished all but a few targets, and I'm doing the clean-up on some others. As for you, Mr. Bartell, I have no need for you. You are not even a good person to keep around as a bargaining chip…like I would need one…and I'm not the hostage-taking type.

You're worthless to me, so if you would be so kind as to step this way you would save me a lot of work."

Cantrell waved the gun at Bartell, and he complied. "That's great, Mr. Bartell. Please follow me. Don't even think of running. I will cut you down before you make it three steps. Cooperation is your best chance here. You do understand that, right Don?" He nodded slowly as he followed Cantrell through the house to a small doorway that led into a garage. Cantrell stepped to the side and motioned with the gun for Bartell to enter. Don stepped off the threshold of the doorway and could hear the sound of plastic under his feet. "A little farther in, please, Don." Don complied until he was facing a large sheet of thick clear plastic at the far end of the garage. "Turn around, please." He did as asked. "Do you have any children, Don?" He shook his head. "Are you married?" "He shook his head again." "It's quite unusual to meet a man your age…what are you? Sixty three?" "Um…sixty four," Bartell said, his voice trembling. "WOW…that old, never married, and no kids. Never been married?" He shook his head. "Are you gay?" Bartell shook his head again. "Damn, Don. Do you have any family who would miss you?"

Bartell began to shake violently and fell to his knees. "Oh God, please, I have no one. I mean you no harm, Garrison. I had nothing to do with what happened to you. I'm just doing my job. For the love of God, please don't kill me." Cantrell lowered the gun to his side and said, "I never meant for anyone but those on the list to come to harm, Don. I never intended for this to happen. I feel just terrible about all of it." Cantrell raised the gun and fired one shot between Bartell's eyes, and his head jerked back and blood splattered onto the plastic behind him. He stood for several seconds just staring at Garrison. He stood there. His eyes fixed on his shooter and asked, "Why Garrison? Why did you do that to me?" Cantrell stood speechless but only for a moment. "I must have split the hemispheres with that shot. Damn. You're one lucky fuckin' guy, Don. One in a million people could have survived that."

Bartell started to walk toward Cantrell, and he said, "One in a million, Don, but not two, and he fired again. Bartell crumpled to the floor. His skull laid open and brain matter was all over the plastic. Garrison took down the sheeting and wrapped up Bartell's body then drug it out to a compost heap that he had in the rear of his home. He opened the large box and picked up Bartell's body and threw it into the dark canister.

He closed the lid and walked back into the house. He left everything as it was. The garage was clean, no sign of the killing. He put up more plastic, walked inside, grabbed a beverage from the refrigerator, and took a drink. He looked at his watch. It was midnight. He said, "Well, now is as good a time as any to wake Rick and Vince. It's time for them to die." He walked out the front door and around the corner to his car and headed for Sherman Oaks.

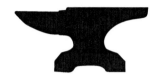

CHAPTER EIGHTEEN

"Where does this lead?"
Sara said, "To the pits of hell!"

The air was still, and the lights of the San Fernando Valley shimmered in the early morning darkness. It was half past two a.m., and Jim, Charlie, and Steve had parked a few blocks down from Rick and Vince's home. "Nice neighborhood," Jim said. Charlie let out a sigh and said, "Yea, this area is pretty sparse, not a lot of rebuilding after the fires. I have a house a few blocks away." "You would rebuild in a neighborhood of faggots?" Jim asked with a chuckle. "They are actually really good neighbors, and when I'm home that's what I want, quiet mother fuckin' neighbors." Jim helped Steve get out of the car and into his wheelchair.

Jim looked at Steve and asked, "Are you sure you want to get into this? You can't run, and I could end up getting killed trying to keep you alive." Steve nodded and said, "You don't have to worry about me. I can still stand if I really, really have to. I have been practicing when Gail's not around. It's hard, but as of yesterday morning I was still able to pull myself up out of this chair."

Jim said, "Great. You can't run or walk, but you can stand… that's just fuckin' great, Steve. So you will be able to make yourself a larger target for the killer." Charlie pointed to some rocks that were near Rick and Vince's home and a stand of trees across the street. "I would bet that our killer is going to take up a sniper position over in those trees. I will cover the front of the house from there." Jim looked around and asked, "What the fuck makes you think he won't come from the back?" Charlie laughed quietly. "For a white boy who fought in the Marine Corps, you sure have forgotten a lot of your training. The back of this house is a steep hillside. The shooter is at a disadvantage trying to shoot from that angle. This guy's advantage in all of his killings with his sniper rifle is elevation. This asshole has the advantage of the cover of night, and I will assume camouflage and night vision to keep out of sight."

Jim went to say something, and Charlie said, "Look, O'Brian, do you want to stand here talking as open targets, or do you want to get your ass into position and some cover? The last I heard you were whining about getting shot. Well, if you want to get shot again and not survive, stand here in the open and argue. I'm going to take a position in those trees." Charlie moved across the street and disappeared. Steve and Jim moved down a long driveway that led to the main house. There was a large stand of bushes in view of the front door and the windows to the house. The two men moved into position, and Steve asked, "Are we going to wake them or just sit here with our cocks in our hands?" Jim frowned and looked at the front entrance to see where he could rouse the two men inside when the lights in one of the rooms came on. "Well, we don't have to worry about waking them." Steve nodded, and Jim told him to stay undercover while he made his way to the front door. Steve sat silent as Jim moved down the drive in the darkness to the house.

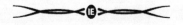

The Eagle watched and waited for the woman he heard talking to El Compo to appear in the room. It wasn't long before the door opened and in walked a too familiar face. Mary Rogers had entered the room. Stunned, the Eagle stood staring as Mary made her way through the stable of girls. She walked up to the girls on their stomachs that had just been branded and smacked them on their brands. There were cries and weeping, and she told them in a quiet whisper in Spanish to be silent or die. The Eagle pulled out a tranquilizer gun and pointed it at Mary. She looked up as the Eagle pushed the door open. She never got a word out before hearing the sound of the gun and the thud of the dart striking her abdomen. The Eagle approached, and she was still conscious. "Really, counselor? You're in on this mess? You're helping this man sell women into sexual servitude, slavery, and prostitution?" Mary looked into the dead eyes of the Eagle and said, "How did you find me?" "I didn't find you. You found me. I'm after Mr. El Compo. You're just the icing on the cake of this citywide corruption."

Mary was passing out when she asked, "Who…are…you?" "How rude of me. Allow me to introduce myself. I am the Iron Eagle." Mary's face turned to horror as she slid down onto her side, and her head rested on the back of one of the branded girls. The Eagle threw her over his shoulder and took her to the laundry room where he bound her and hid her in a laundry hamper. He walked back into the room and made his way back to the upper door. He went to push the door open when it opened on its own. He moved back behind the opening door, which hid him as it swung open, and he waited for the person on the other side.

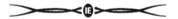

Charlie had made his way up the hillside across from the house and saw some concrete steps. He moved up to the top of them to find the burned out remains of a home. He could also see several skeletal remains near a masonry fireplace. He looked at them and whispered to himself, "Well, I can take the Marks' off the missing person's board." He looked around and saw another set of concrete stairs that led higher onto the property.

Charlie knew Emily and Scott Marks well. He had been to their home many times through the years. They were both university professors and were well known for their parties. Charlie knew that those stairs led to a large concrete patio that the Marks' had built several decades earlier. It would be the perfect vantage point to look down on the house. He started up the steep steps to gain an advantage on the killer.

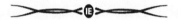

Ricardo Pina had woken early as was his norm after a night of rough sex. He and Vince had made a pact when they became a couple that they were both tops, and that they both gave each other pleasure, and that included each allowing the other anal sex. Vince had a large cock, and when Ricardo had to take him, he always ended up in pain and unable to sleep. And last night had been his night to be the 'cushion.' Rick walked bowed legged into the kitchen and poured himself a shot of whisky and drank it quickly. He grimaced as the liquor ran into his mouth and down his sore throat where Vince's cock had been only an hour earlier. The whisky numbed his throat, and he took a second shot, and the pain started to dissipate.

Vince walked nude into the kitchen and said, "I'm sorry, Rick. I forget how hard I am on you." Rick was leaning against the counter in the kitchen and said, "It's not your fault, honey. It's been our agreement for ten years. I can handle you in my ass once I dilate, then it's heaven. You came hard tonight. It's the aftermath that takes me a day or so to get over." Vince walked over and grabbed Rick's cock and kissed him, then moved down and started to give him head. Vince stood up and said, "Come back to bed. I will take one for the team, big guy. That always makes you feel better." They smiled, and Rick handed Vince a shot of whisky and said, "Now that's an invitation too good to turn down. I'm going to pound you hard!" Vince shot the whisky and said as he grimaced while swallowing the liquor, "I... would...expect...nothing less. Punish my ass!"

Jim could see the two men through the front window, and he saw more than he wanted to. He watched as the two men held hands and started across the living room to what he could only assume was the bedroom. There were no curtains, and Jim knew why. The house was set down off the road. There would be no way to see in unless you were high up at the right angle. Jim was getting ready to move for the front door when he heard the crack of glass. He looked in to see Vince and Rick both standing almost frozen. There was a second crack, and Jim watched helplessly as Vince and Patrick fell to the floor in their living room. Jim looked back up the hill into the darkness of the trees where Charlie had gone. He started back toward Steve through the darkness, and when he got to him Steve asked, "What the fuck just happened?" "Sniper." Steve looked around and said, "Then he has night vision, and if he has night vision he sees us." Jim nodded. There was a moment without movement when suddenly Steve rolled his wheelchair into the middle of the driveway.

He waved his arms. He was wearing an FBI windbreaker, and with what breath he could draw said, "I'm a cop, you son of a bitch. Go ahead and shoot me. Let's take this to the federal level!" Jim ran out and grabbed the wheelchair and started to push Steve back when a voice called out from the darkness.

"I know you want to catch me, but you're not going to. I have no beef with the FBI or the sheriff's department. This is personal, and I have two targets left. I know that Captain Boyd is still alive. One of my men was killed in the gas explosion at his home. While it saddens me that I lost a comrade, he wasn't paying attention, and the Eagle got him." Jim and Steve looked at each other as the shooter continued. "Yes...I know that the Iron Eagle is hunting me. I also know that he has one of my men, and that he is saving the victims of some of the others. I mean him no harm either. He does what he does, and I do what I do. The Iron Eagle is safe unless he tries to stop me, and if he does, I will gladly trade my life for his. I know you know the Eagle, Sheriff. Please let him know I wish him no

harm. Now, if you will excuse me, I need to deal with Mr. Boyd and with LAPD Police Chief Albert Ralston. Who will I take out first? Hmm....I guess you will just have to wait and see."

It grew quiet, and a shot interrupted the darkness. Jim locked the brakes on Steve's wheelchair and took off up the drive and across the street to the concrete steps that Charlie had headed for. Jim ran as fast as he could. He was running on pure adrenaline. He reached the top of the stairs, and saw Charlie on the ground. Jim ran over and called out, "Charlie, fuck, Charlie?" Jim got to him, and Charlie raised his head and said, "I hit him in the right shoulder. I hit the white son of a bitch in the shoulder, Jim. He's wounded." Jim pulled a small Maglite off his belt and shined it down onto Charlie. "Jesus Christ, Charlie, you're hit." He could see that Charlie had been shot in the chest, and he could also tell that he was not wearing his vest. "Jesus Christ, Charlie! You don't have your vest on." "Who needs a vest when I'm shining a seat with my nigger ass."

Charlie let out a light laugh. Jim had lifted him into his arms, and Charlie was lying across Jim's arms and knees. Charlie looked up at Jim and said, "Ain't this a bitch? The last person I'm going to see in this life is your whitey ginger face!" Jim looked down into Charlie's dying eyes, and as he released his last breath, Jim said, "Oh go fuck yourself!" Charlie's last words to Jim were, "I already did!" Jim held Charlie's lifeless body in his arms as he heard Steve calling to him in the darkness and the sound of sirens in the distance. Steve had called 911 and sent out a distress call. Jim laid Charlie down on the burnt out remains of the house and said, "I'm sorry I have to leave you like this. I have to get this son of a bitch, especially if you wounded him."

Jim stood up and walked down the stairs and across the street to Steve who had managed to release the brakes on his chair and wheel his way to the top of the drive. The first units arrived on scene, and Jim shouted out orders and directions to Charlie's body then pushed Steve to his car. Jim took out a coin and said, "There are two guys left alive on this asshole's list. Heads we go and try to save Ralston, tails we try to save

Boyd." Jim tossed the coin in the air and told Steve to call it. "Heads…
Boyd's an asshole who deserves to die." The coin landed on the street,
and Jim pointed his flashlight at it. Steve said, "We better get going. The
fucking killer's got a head start to Ralston's house." Jim put Steve in the
car, started the engine, and sped off down the street to Ventura Boulevard
and the 101 Freeway in the hopes of saving Ralston.

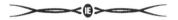

Sara was sitting on one of the sofas as the girls looked on. Barbara
knew why they were there. Gail had a suspicious look on her face,
but Jade was half asleep and clueless. "What the fuck is so important
to get me out of bed at quarter to three?" Jade asked, "haven't I had
enough drama for one night?" Barbara got up and poured a round of
drinks for all of the women. She put them on a silver serving tray
and walked to the living room table and sat the drinks down in front
of the girls. Sara, Gail, and Barbara all took their drinks and swigged
them down. Jade looked on at the girls then the drink and picked
it up and asked, "What the fuck are we drinking to?" Sara grabbed
a bottle of Nadurra scotch from the bar and a full ice bucket and
refreshed all of the drinks.

Jade was more alert after the drink and asked, "What…am…I…
here…for? I know it's not to have a friendly drink." Barbara said, "The
Iron Eagle needs our help." Sara shot Barb a look, and Barb looked
back and said, "What? Were you going to wait all fuckin' night, Sara?"
Jade looked scared and asked Sara, "You help the Iron Eagle?" Sara
nodded slowly, taking a drink of her scotch. Jade looked at Barbara and
asked, "You know who the Eagle is?" Barbara nodded as well. Jade
looked at Gail and asked, "Do you know who the Iron Eagle is?" She
shook her head. Sara sat down and said, "The Eagle is on the hunt right
now. He has two people in his custody who are very, very bad men, and
there are about ten young girls who have been kidnapped that the Eagle
and his men saved that need medical attention."

Jade said, "Men…THE Iron Eagle has men…men who know who he is?" Barbara laughed and told Jade, "No. They have no fuckin' clue who the Eagle is. They just wait by the phone, and he calls them when he needs them…like Charlie's Angels used to do on that TV show in the seventies." That got a laugh from everyone but Jade. She looked at Sara and said, "You took an oath. I took an oath to do no harm." Sara sipped her drink and said, "Yea, that's an easy oath to uphold until you've been on the victim's side of the people the Iron Eagle captures." Jade took a drink and asked in a low, quiet voice, "It's John…John's the Iron Eagle?" Sara nodded slowly as did Barbara, but Gail sat silent.

Jade said, "Jesus Christ. It all makes sense now. Why the hell couldn't I see it? Fuck. It's been John all of these years." Sara said, "John and the Eagle are two very separate and distinct personalities." Jade smarted off and said, "So, he's schizo?" "My husband is perfectly sane, and millions of people are alive today as a result of his actions. Be careful how you speak of my husband and your protector. You don't want to insult your way to the other side of him or us."

Jade looked shocked and said, "It was meant as a joke." "It wasn't funny," said Barbara, "now there are some very injured young girls, and Sara needs help. Are you going to help us, or do we need to send you home?" Jade looked on and said to Sara, "I'm sorry. I will help you. How bad could it be?" Sara just shook her head and said, "You, Jade, have been happily protected from the savagery of these killers. I know you see the aftermath on your autopsy table, but here you see the road that put men, women, and children on your table to begin with. If you think you're ready for what you're about to see, I promise you you're not."

Sara walked over to a wall off the entrance to the house and put her hand on it, and it slid open. Barbara and Gail got up and followed. Jade stood up and walked hesitantly behind the girls and asked, "Where does this lead?" Sara said, "To the pits of hell!"

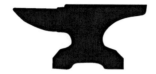

CHAPTER NINETEEN

"Mexicans are no
better than animals."

The door to the dungeon in Mark's home swung open, hiding the Eagle. Mark and two other men entered calling Mary's name. The Eagle pulled a tranquilizer gun from his chest and slowly pushed the door, slipping two darts into the magazine clip and pulling back the barrel to put one in the tube. The sound of the door closing behind the three men startled them, and they turned. The two men flanking El Compo drew their weapons, but the Eagle shot them, and they fell immediately. The girls screamed, and El Compo stared into the cold dead eyes of the Eagle as he approached.

"Please...please...I'm begging you...it was only business. I never intended to hurt anyone. I gave them lives, homes, and work. Mexicans are no better than animals. The women are hard workers and very, very obedient sex slaves when trained."

The Eagle reached out his arm and grabbed Mark by the throat. The girls sat in silence as the Eagle took out a field knife from his pants and cut off Mark's pants and underwear and threw him on the ground.

He pressed his boot into Mark's back. The man thrashed beneath his boot but could not free himself. He screamed for help as the Eagle pressed his face against the concrete floor. His screams were loud, and the Eagle pulled a Glock with a silencer on it from a holster and stood and watched the entrance door. In seconds, three heavily armed men came bounding in. The Eagle dropped each man with a single shot to the head. There were screams from the girls, and the Eagle put his finger to his lips and said in Spanish, "Silence, unless you want them to kill you." The screams stopped. "How many more guards?" the Eagle asked with his foot firmly planted on Mark's head. "I don't know." The Eagle drug him over to the fire pit and threw him down on the ground. He pressed his boot into Mark's back and said, "If there were others nearby, they would already be here."

Mark murmured something, and the Eagle grabbed one of the branding irons from the fire and pressed it into Mark's ass. He screamed in agony. The Eagle leaned down and whispered into his ear, never taking his eyes off the door, "We've only just begun." Then he took another branding iron and pressed it against El Compo's back. His screams were blood curdling, and the Eagle allowed it while watching the door and waiting.

After five minutes, he grabbed Mark by the hair and threw him across the room, sending his body slamming into the steel door that led to the laundry room. "I guess we have no more guests." The Eagle pushed Mark onto his stomach and zip tied his hands and feet then opened the door and the laundry basket that held Mary.

Mark saw her face and started to scream again, so the Eagle pulled out the tranquilizer gun and shot him in the neck. "I have heard enough from you for now." The Eagle pulled his tablet and sent a text to C4 and Cosmo. The response was that they were in position. He gave them the coordinates to the back entrance and the laundry room, and the two men were there within seconds. Cosmo looked around and said, "Fuck... what is this, dude? A slave trader?" The Eagle nodded and said, "Free the girls. I doubt that many of them can walk."

Lance and Patrick worked with the Eagle to free all the girls. Then the men took the girls two by two over their shoulders and followed the Eagle to the van. When the last girl was in, the Eagle dropped Mary and Mark in the back. "C4, have you set the charges?" "Yea…I have them set to the wireless signal on my cell." The Eagle ordered everyone into the van and drove away from the house slowly with his lights off. When they were over a hundred yards away, the three men got out of the van and walked to the back of it.

Music and laughter could be heard coming from the well lit home. The Eagle looked at C4 and said, "They came to buy slaves and abuse women – on my mark." C4 had the phone in his hand with his finger on the call button. The Eagle looked at the young girls in the back of the van in different degrees of injury. He opened the door and said to them in Spanish, "You don't want to see this," then he closed the door and said, "MAY GOD NOT HAVE MERCY ON YOUR SOULS!" He nodded to C4 who pressed the button on the phone, and the house exploded.

It lit up the night sky as the house fell over the side of the cliff nearly a thousand feet, taking all of those inside with it. The Eagle turned to Lance and Patrick and asked, "Did you bring my truck?" "Yea. It's parked up the road," Lance said. "Okay. Please take these women to my lair and make sure that Mr. El Compo and Ms. Rogers are placed in isolation. Sara will know what to do." Patrick asked, "Do you need us for anything else." The Eagle shook his head. "No…once you have dropped off the girls and these two, go home. I will call if I need you. There is only one person left to get, and that's the ring leader of this killing spree and slavery and drug ring, and I have a pretty damn good idea who it is now."

The men headed for Malibu, and the Eagle threw his bags in the truck and called Jim. The phone was ringing, and Jim answered. "Charlie is dead, so are Pina and Espeno. The killer is going after Boyd or Ralston." "How long ago did this happen?" the Eagle asked. "Ten minutes. The scene is a mess. Steve and I are in the car, and we are heading to Ralston's home. Were you able to take care of Boyd and El Compo?" "Yes…I got El Compo, but Boyd is still alive. I have the girls that were coming in.

I also have El Compo and a special guest on their way to my lair." Jim coughed and said, "You might as well tell me who it is because I have a feeling one of us won't be coming back. The killer called to me from his sniper position and said that he is willing to trade his life for his targets. He also told me that while he has no intention of killing me, Steve, or the Iron Eagle, if you get in his way he will kill you."

There was a moment of silence, and the Eagle said, "The killer is Cantrell!" Jim asked, "How the fuck did you figure that out?" "Process of elimination. A sniper took down Chilton in front of his home a few hours ago. He also killed Chilton's wife. I got it over the radio on my way here. I'm pretty certain that Cantrell has Ralston." Jim asked, "You don't think he's just going to kill Ralston like the rest of the victims?" "No…he's going to grandstand. He will want an audience." "Where the fuck is this dumb ass going to get an audience at almost four a.m.?" Jim asked. "Cantrell will take Ralston to City Walk in Universal City where he will have an audience with all of the live camera feeds. He will set up Ralston for public execution. Where are you?" the Eagle asked. "Steve and I are in the San Fernando Valley, which has really become death's valley for cops." "I'm in Bel-Air. I can be at City Walk in five minutes. You and Steve go back to the house. I will meet you back there." Jim said, "Oh no…that fucker killed one of my best friends. He's going down…Charlie died in my arms. I want blood." "If you go out there, you are going to get blood, only it's going to be yours or mine," the Eagle said, and Jim replied, "I'm en route."

Jim hung up the line, and Steve asked, "So, what's the deal?" "The Eagle says that Garrison Cantrell is the head of this killing spree. He thinks that he will publicly execute Ralston at City Walk in Universal City." Steve nodded slowly and said in a weak voice, "He's right…we have to get there. It will be an ambush. Cantrell is baiting the Eagle into a trap." Jim sped down the 101 Freeway headed for Universal City and its well known public venue.

><====<▣>====<

Patrick and Lance drove into the underground tunnel at the Eagle's lair at four a.m. They pulled in, and Patrick went into the lair to find Sara, Barbara, Jade, and Gail treating the girls they picked up in Woodland Hills. Patrick said, "We have another van load of girls, Sara." Jade looked up, teary eyed, and Sara said, "Bring them in. How many?" Lance was walking in with two girls over his shoulders, and Patrick said, "In all of the confusion at the house I really don't know." Sara said to put them on the couches and on the rug in the foyer, so they could be as comfortable as possible. He nodded and walked out to the garage.

Jade asked, "Where the hell are the Eagle, Jim, and Steve?" Sara was putting a cool compress on a brand on one of the first girls that had been brought to the lair and said, "They are together, no doubt dispensing justice or getting ahold of the person or people who need justice dispensed to them." "When will we see them?" Barbara answered, "We will see them when we see them, if we ever see them again."

Jade's face dropped and tears began to run down her cheeks as girl after girl was brought to the foyer. All of them were injured, and she could smell the burnt flesh of their brands. She could see fear and pain in the faces of all of them. Jade asked, "What type of animal would do this to another human being?" Sara was working feverishly and said, "If the Eagle has his way, you will get to look into the eyes of the evil person who is responsible for this, and God only knows what else." Jade went back to work as Patrick and Lance kept bringing in the girls, tears of sadness and rage running down her face.

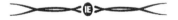

The Eagle got to City Walk at just after four a.m. He parked in a far parking lot in a darkened corner and grabbed a bag and reloaded his tranquilizer gun and put a new clip in his Glock and extras in his pockets. He moved through the darkness toward a ladder that he saw that would allow him access to the roof. He saw no other vehicles but also no signs of life. The area was patrolled twenty-four seven by

LAPD and private security. He knew by the silence and the lack of police that Cantrell was already there and had Ralston and would use him as bait to get him into the open. The Eagle moved to the ladder and saw that the lock on it had been broken. "Cantrell used this to climb up," he said to himself as he quietly pulled the ladder down and began to climb up to the rooftop five stories above him.

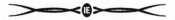

Jim came barreling into the parking lot at Universal City Walk through two downed gates and skidded to a stop near the entrance. Steve looked over at Jim and said, "Subtle…really fuckin' subtle. You think that Cantrell knows we're here?" Jim opened the car door and said, "I want the mother fucker to know we're here," Jim yelled as he got out of the car. He pulled Steve's wheelchair from the back seat and helped him get into it. Once Steve was set, Jim said "This is a handicap-friendly place. You should be able to get around. Are you strong enough?" Steve nodded, and Jim took off through the well lit entrance to the main square. Steve was weak, and he slowly pushed his wheelchair up the entrance walk, knowing that he was an easy and open target if the killer was there and decided to kill him.

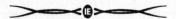

Garrison Cantrell heard the squealing tires of Jim's car in the distance as he put the last of the zip tie hand cuffs on the officers he had taken down. There were eight men in LAPD uniform on their knees in front of him with their backs to him and ten private security guards in front of the LAPD officers. Cantrell pulled his Glock with the silencer on it and put it to the back of the first officer's head in the line. "I'm afraid I don't have time for speeches, so I will have to dispense with the explanations."

Cantrell walked behind officer after officer and shot them point blank in the back of the head. Each body hit the floor of the storage

room. Some were flopping on the ground in front of the private security guards and others just dropped like a bag of bricks. For those still moving, Cantrell put an extra bullet in their heads. Blood and brains pooled on the floor in front of the private security guards, and he said, "Relax. I am not going to kill private sector security personnel...unless...any of you are off duty LAPD."

There were wild eyes from all of the men who had duct tape over their mouths. "Hell, I can't risk it..." Cantrell said and started shooting the other guards. He walked up to the last guard as five others flopped around on the ground. He looked him in the eye, and the guard stared back with an icy stare. Cantrell let out a laugh and said, "Now, I know you're definitely off duty LAPD. Trying to make a buck, aren't you?" The guard just glared at Cantrell. "Jesus, it's a bloodbath in here." He kicked the final guard in the stomach and rolled him to the middle of the floor and pushed him through the blood, brains, and bone fragments.

"Oh yeah...you're LAPD all right. You like the blood of your fellow officers all over your body, you piece of shit?" Cantrell was wild-eyed, and he kicked the officer as the two men slid around in the blood and bodily fluids of the others. Cantrell slipped while trying to kick the guard again and fell on top of him and then onto the blood covered floor. Cantrell had totally lost track of what he had come there to do. He was obsessed with torturing that final guard, certain that he was off duty LAPD.

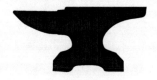

CHAPTER TWENTY

"Son of a fuckin' bitch, not again!"

T he Eagle made his way along the rooftop following a trail of disturbed roof gravel used to help insulate against the hot valley days. The Eagle moved between rooftop air conditioning units and followed the trail until it ended near a walkway. The Eagle could see that Cantrell was dragging something with him, and he could only assume that it was LAPD Police Chief Albert Ralston. The Eagle looked down into the middle of a quad where there was a circle of shops all around, but there was no movement and no noise. He moved out onto the rooftop covering and saw Jim running up the walk yelling for Cantrell. "Fuck," the Eagle said to himself as Jim slowed to a walk screaming Cantrell's name.

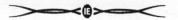

Steve had wheeled himself up the walk and could hear Jim yelling in the distance. He knew that Cantrell was insane, and at the moment so was Jim. Steve moved his wheelchair through the darkness until he was

near the center circle of the quad where the shops were clustered. He knew that he was in the heart of the place, and that this is where it was all going to happen. He rolled into a dark corner until his wheelchair was stopped by something. He looked down, and there was a dark object at his feet. He pulled a small Maglite from his top pocket and shined it at the object, only to see Albert Ralston at the foot of his wheelchair. Steve pushed himself back and was able to grab ahold of a fire extinguisher next to his chair, and he lifted himself out of the wheelchair but fell to the ground next to Ralston. He took the light and shined it at Ralston's face. He was alive and alert. He had duct tape over his mouth and zip ties around his wrists and ankles.

Steve pulled himself up next to Ralston and said, "Chief Ralston, my name is Special Agent Steve Hoffman FBI. I'm not alone. We know who took you, and we know what his plans are. I'm going to cut these ties, but whatever you do don't try to make a break for it because you will end up in the crosshairs of friendly fire. There are men on the roof and men on the ground." Jim's voice could be heard screaming Cantrell's name off in the distance.

"Sheriff O'Brian is attempting to get Cantrell's attention and lure him out, so we can drop him. Do you understand me?" Ralston nodded calmly, and Steve removed the tape from Ralston's mouth, and there was some material inside his mouth. Steve pulled it out, and Ralston said, "Is this a bitch or what? Fuck! You become the chief of police, and everyone thinks you're responsible for the ills of a whole damn department." Steve moved down and cut the zip ties, and Albert sat up as did Steve, and he asked, "So what now, Agent Hoffman?" "We are going to slip out of this area. There is an elevator just over to our left. I'm going to need your help standing up." Ralston helped Steve up, and he leaned him against a pillar near the center of the quad. Steve said, "Now, you get over to the elevator and take it down to the ground floor and wait for back up." Ralston looked at Steve and said, "What about you?" "I will be fine. He's only looking to kill LAPD. I had a run in with him earlier tonight. He's not looking to kill me, but he wants to kill you. Now…get going."

Albert moved across the quad and pressed the button for the elevator. In a matter of seconds, Steve heard it ding, and the light of the elevator lit up the area. The doors closed, and Steve was alone.

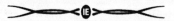

Cantrell heard Jim's voice calling his name from the distance. He slipped and slid in the blood and fought to get his footing. He was covered in blood as was the security guard on the ground at his feet. "You get a stay of execution while I deal with Sheriff O'Brian," Cantrell said, making his way out of the storage closet and out to the quad. He ran to a nearby ladder and climbed up onto the roof. He was raging angry and talking to himself the whole way. He moved on his stomach on the white roof that glowed bright in the moonlight, and he moved to the edge of the roof covering with a high-powered rifle in his hands. He heard Jim yelling and cursing as he walked in his direction.

"Where are you, you son of a bitch? Get your ass out here, and I will clean the fuckin' ground with you." Jim was screaming at the top of his lungs. He was walking freely in the moonlight…an easy target for anyone. He had his weapon out, and he was waving it in the air, taunting Cantrell.

Cantrell let out a laugh, not loud enough for Jim to hear, but loud enough for the Eagle to hear just two rooftops over. The Eagle crawled to the edge of the roof but could not get a good shot at Cantrell. He could see Jim walking right into an ambush, and there was nothing he could do to stop it without giving away his position. The Eagle grabbed his tranquilizer gun from his hip and aimed it at Jim. He had the angle on Jim and took the shot. Jim stopped, looked around, and then said, "Son of a fuckin' bitch, not again!" and collapsed onto the ground.

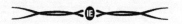

Cantrell had Jim in his sights and was about to pull the trigger when he saw him collapse. He let out a slight laugh and said, "You had a fuckin' heart attack, you dumb ass. Now, if you're here, so is the damn Eagle." Cantrell put his eye into the scope and began to scan the ground. The Eagle saw Cantrell and pushed himself up on his knees and then to his feet and moved silently from rooftop to rooftop until he and Cantrell were on the same walkway covering.

The Eagle laid down and began to crawl silently in Cantrell's direction. Jim started to kick his leg as he began to come to, and Cantrell saw it but wasn't concerned. The Eagle watched as Cantrell moved the scope side to side and then stopped. The Eagle knew Cantrell had locked on a target.

The Eagle had pulled out his tranquilizer gun and was moving to aim it at him when Cantrell said, "If it's not the Iron fuckin' Eagle. I told the sheriff and the FBI agent with him that I bear you no ill will, and I had no intention of killing you unless you tried to stop me, and I can see that you are indeed here to do so." The Eagle raised the tranquilizer gun and fired, striking Cantrell in the back of the leg. He jerked but stayed focused on his target. The Eagle heard a soft sound emanate from Cantrell's weapon and realized that Cantrell had fired. The Eagle moved fast to take control of him and saw the pant legs of a figure shrouded in darkness.

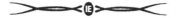

Jim was coming to but was way too woozy to move or say anything. He heard the sound of a bell like that of an elevator and saw a dark figure moving in the direction of Cantrell's voice. He heard Cantrell calling out to the Eagle, but he was confused. He tried to reach for his weapon but collapsed back down onto the concrete and was out cold.

Albert Ralston had gotten on the elevator and then off. He remained on the main level with Steve. He heard Cantrell yelling and calling out to the Iron Eagle. He moved in the darkness back to where Steve had

released him, but Steve was gone. Ralston was half in moonlight and half darkness when he heard what sounded like a puff of air. He knew immediately it was the sound of a silencer on a fired weapon.

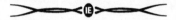

Sara was barking out instructions to the girls as she was trying to help the victims of Mark El Compo and Mary Rogers. Barbara restrained Mark and Mary together in operating room number two until the Eagle decided where he wanted them. Gail had no medical education, but she was trying to help one of the girls who was bleeding profusely from her side. She called out to Sara and said, "Sara, this poor girl is bleeding from her side. I don't know what to do." Sara said, "Jade, get to Gail. See what the cause of the bleed is and see if you can stop it."

Jade ran across the room to Gail who was on her knees in a puddle of blood. "Oh shit, Sara. It looks like this is an old wound that has reopened just above this kid's right kidney." Sara asked if she could cauterize it. "Jesus Christ, Sara. I don't even know where the bleed is. She's losing blood fast." Sara yelled to Barbara who was tending to two other girls and said, "Barb, go to the fridge in OR one. You will find O negative in the right hand sliding drawer of the unit. Grab three of them and an IV bag then grab an IV kit from the top shelf and bring it to Jade, stat." Barbara jumped up and disappeared and was back in less than a minute with everything that Sara had asked for.

Jade said, "Sara, I can't see shit…" Sara ran over, and she and Barbara grabbed the girl under her arms and carried her to OR three. Jade was hot on their heels with everything that Barbara had brought her. As they walked down the hall, Jade saw the bloody hands and feet of Alverez who was in a sitting position on a gurney, mumbling in agony. She saw two other people strapped down in another room, and then she followed Sara and Barbara into the operating room and helped them get the girl on the gurney. She was still bleeding profusely, and Sara placed a heart rate monitor on her finger. She barely had a pulse.

Sara called Jade and said, "There's no time to scrub. Pull that table next to you over." Jade pulled over a steel tray that had scalpels and silk thread for sutures and handed items to Sara as she ordered them. Barbara started an IV and got the blood going while Sara operated. Jade was in a cloud and lost herself for a moment. Sara yelled out and said, "Jade, are you a goddamn doctor or not?"

Jade snapped out of it and handed her another instrument while responding, "I'm sorry. I'm always dealing with death, not ever trying to save lives." "Well, welcome to the other side. It is my life's work to keep people alive…" Sara paused, "most of the time." Jade shivered as she watched Sara work, and after ten minutes of operating she had stopped the bleeding, and the girl had stabilized. Sara said, "That's a quick fix. We have to get her to the hospital." Barbara said, "We have to wait for the Eagle." Sara nodded, and the three women walked out of the operating room, leaving the girl in stable condition.

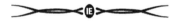

The Eagle cuffed and hog tied Cantrell and was looking over the edge of the roof when he saw a man step out from the darkness near the legs on the ground. He called out, and the man looked up. Jim was sitting up and started to push himself up all the while calling Cantrell's name. The Eagle called out to Jim and said, "Cantrell is down, Jim. I have him. Someone is down on the ground. Cantrell got off a shot after I darted him. He thought he was shooting at me." Jim got to the edge of the landing and walked into the darkness, and the Eagle heard him cry out, "NO…NO…NO!"

The Eagle grabbed the edge of the roof covering and dropped to the ground and ran over to where Jim was calling out. There, on the ground, half lit and half in darkness was Steve Hoffman with a bullet wound to his chest. He was gasping for air, and Jim was holding him in his arms. The Eagle was standing next to the man he saw from the roof and said, "Chief Ralston, I assume?" Ralston nodded. The Eagle

took out his tranquilizer gun and shot Ralston in the chest. The Eagle said, "I'm sorry for this, but it's for your own protection."

The Eagle took off his mask and looked into Steve's eyes and asked, "Why, Steve? What were you thinking?" Steve coughed a little and said, "To keep the Iron Eagle alive. I saw you behind Cantrell. I knew he would kill you. It's okay. It doesn't hurt anymore." Steve's eyes dilated as Jim held him in his arms. John hung his head down, and a tear dripped onto Steve's hand. Jim said, "We are not leaving him here, John." "No, Jim. We are not. Let me get Cantrell. We can call this in. I will zip tie Ralston, and we will take Steve home."

Jim held Steve close as the Eagle moved to get Cantrell's unconscious body off the roof. When he made it down and back to Jim, he threw Cantrell on the ground and said, "Get Steve's wheelchair." Jim found it only a few feet away and rolled it over to John who was holding Steve in his arms as a father would hold a child. John gently sat Steve in the chair and said, "Take him down to your car and head for Malibu." Jim looked on and said, "What are you going to do?" Jim could see that the line between the Eagle and John was now blurred. Jim didn't know if he was talking to John or the Eagle, and he could tell the same was the situation for John. The Eagle pulled his mask back on and said, "I will be behind you with Cantrell. I have to check and see if there are other casualties." Jim turned, pushing Steve's body in the wheelchair slowly back to the parking lot as the Eagle ran through the quad looking for survivors. He was about to climb up the ladder that Cantrell had been lying in front of when he heard a faint male voice calling out for help. The Eagle listened and followed the sound of the voice until he got to the doorway that was marked 'Storage.' He pushed the door open, but there was no light. He felt for a switch and found it. He turned on the light and saw one of the most gruesome scenes he had ever encountered.

There was a sea of bodies, some in LAPD uniforms, and others in gray uniforms. All were head shot, and blood and skull fragments were everywhere. The Eagle grabbed a pair of cleaning booties from a shelf and put them on his feet. He tried not to slip as he made his way through the

piles of corpses looking for any sign of life. He was about to leave when he heard a murmur and saw one of the bodies move. He pulled the body over, and there was an uninjured officer underneath one of the corpses.

The Eagle grabbed the man who was bound and covered in blood, and the guard started to stammer and stutter incoherently. "You're safe. He won't be coming back," the Eagle said. The officer said, "He just kept killing, one after another after another. The more he killed, the more brutal, and the faster he moved to kill the others. He was going to kill me until he heard a voice I heard, too. He said it was the sheriff."

The Eagle shook his head, "It wasn't the sheriff. It was the chief of police who had been abducted and brought here to be killed in a very, very public way. What's your name?" "Robert...Robert Willits." "You're in a security guard uniform. Are you off duty LAPD working here?" He nodded slowly and said, "Yea, I'm a detective out of Hollywood division. I picked up this job to make a few bucks and help out some of my friends here." Willits pointed to the dead bodies and said, "To keep something like this from happening." The Eagle nodded and helped Robert up and walked him out. He marked the door with a black marker with a crime scene line and walked Willits out to where Chief Ralston was lying on a bench. "Is he dead?" The Eagle shook his head and said, "No, just unconscious for his own protection." The sun was starting to rise and cast its light into the shadows. The Eagle looked over to see a pool of blood where Steve had been shot. He looked at his PDA, and it was ten after six.

"What now?" Willits asked the Eagle. "Do you have a cell phone?" Willits nodded. "Call 911. You know what to tell them. You and the chief are the only surviving officers. Get them here and explain what happened, so they can start to work this scene." Willits looked at the Eagle and said, "But I don't really know what happened. Some nut job took all of us hostage and then murdered everyone. How do I explain this?" The Eagle stood up and said, "The scene will explain itself. Make the call." He started to walk off, and Willits asked, "You saved me and the chief. Who are you?" Without looking back, he said, "I'm the Iron Eagle, and on this day I was only able to save a few." Willits looked on

at the hulking figure walking away from him and said, "You saved me and the chief. You saved someone." "This time it wasn't enough." Willits watched as the Eagle disappeared. He pulled his phone and called 911.

The Eagle picked up Cantrell and threw him over his shoulder. He was starting to come to as the Eagle threw him in the back of his truck. He took off his mask, started the truck, and headed for the 405 Freeway and Malibu. Cantrell called out to the Eagle in a groggy voice and asked, "Where am I, and where am I going?" The Eagle said, "You are in the custody of the Iron Eagle, and where you're going is into a literal living hell." Cantrell was screaming in the back of the truck, and the Eagle did nothing to stop him.

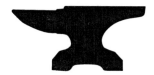

CHAPTER TWENTY-ONE

"Because Mark is unable to make it,
so a friend sent me to finish you."

All was quiet when Brian Boyd pulled up in front of the remains of his home. It was half past nine a.m. He didn't have the whole story, but he knew that the threat had been neutralized. He also knew that only he and the chief of police had survived the night. He looked around at the homes near his own. The windows were blown out of several of them, but there were no injuries. His house had crime scene tape around it, and he showed his ID to an officer on duty, watching over the house and was allowed to pass. Boyd walked onto the concrete where his front door once stood. He walked into the house and walked through the area. There was a yellow tarp in the family room where the remains of Marco Estrada had landed after the explosion. He walked to the backyard, pulled out his cell phone, and called for Mark El Compo. A woman answered the line, and he asked for Mark but was told he was out. He asked when he might be in, and she asked who was calling. He told her his name, but it had no impact on her. Boyd got pissed and said, "You listen to me, bitch, I'm the

only fuckin' cop left who can take care of business for him. If he wants to keep from having an accident, you tell that fucker to call me NOW! I'm the man in charge of the LAPD, and I can make his life a nightmare if he doesn't give me what I want." There were a few moments of silence, then the female voice said, "Mr. El Compo will meet you at the Starbucks at the corner of Reseda Boulevard and Ventura Boulevard in a half hour." "Now that's fuckin' better. You sound like a sweet piece of ass. Tell him to bring you with him. I want a blow job." "As you wish."

The line went dead, and Brian took off as fast as he could to get to the Starbucks in Tarzana. He was excited and said to himself as he drove down Topanga to Ventura Boulevard, "I'm in the catbird seat now, man. Mark will have to deal with me and me alone. If he wants my protection, it's going to be a fifty-fifty split, or I will throw his ass in jail. Jesus, I'm going to be rich, and I can dump Cindy and the rest of the family and start my own fuckin' harem." He sped off to his meeting, smiling from ear to ear.

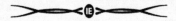

Sara hung up the line and looked over at John, sitting on the edge of a chair in the foyer. John called Lance and Patrick and told them to make sure some harm came to Brian Boyd. They said they would take care of him and hung up. John sat in the foyer with Sara; Jim was sitting off to his right with Barbara next to him. Gail was on her knees in front of the couch where Steve's body lay. She stroked his head. His face was peaceful. Jade stood off in a corner of the room in shock.

Gail asked, "Did he suffer?" John told her no. Gail looked over at Jim for confirmation, and he shook his head in agreement. John looked down at her and said, "I'm sorry, Gail. I had no idea he was in the line of fire." She spoke through the tears and said, "He always looked up to you, John. He told me that finding you was the best thing that ever happened to the Bureau." John was choking back his own tears and said, "He taught me a lot, and I'm proud to have known him. I just wish he hadn't died the way he did. He died saving me." Gail stood up and walked over to John and

said, "I loved Steve with all my heart, John. If there was a way to die for Steve, dying in the line of duty protecting a fellow officer in the face of danger was exactly how he wanted to go. This spared him the indignity of dying a horrible death with ALS. I know that wherever he is, if there is something after this life, he's happy." She leaned in and kissed John on the cheek and went back over to be with Steve.

Jim looked at the room full of people and said, "He was one of my best friends. We walked a lot of roads together. He died doing what he loved, and the fact that he saved Special Agent John Swenson and the Iron Eagle is more than he could have ever hoped for given his illness." Heads nodded around the room, and Jade said, "I don't mean to sound callous, but we need to get Steve on ice. He's decomposing as we speak." John and Jim got angry looks on their faces for only a brief moment, then they realized that Jade was right.

Sara asked, "While everything that you all have said about Steve and what he did is true, how are you going to have him listed as being killed in the line of duty?" Jim and John looked at each other, and John said, "He will be found shot in Cantrell's home." "And what about Cantrell?" Sara asked. "The Eagle will extract a confession from Cantrell that will verify the story, ballistics will match Cantrell's weapon, showing Steve was shot and had fallen in the line of duty. That's the easy part. Living without his presence, far more difficult." No one asked any more questions about what the Eagle was going to do to Cantrell. Jim and John moved to take Steve's body to Cantrell's home and set up the crime scene.

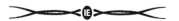

Brian Boyd pulled into the parking lot at Starbucks and looked for Mark's car, but he didn't see it. He figured he was early, so he got out of his unmarked police cruiser and walked into the shop. He ordered a cappuccino and waited for his name to be called while he looked around for Mark. The place was jammed with morning regulars all getting their coffee fix before heading off for their day's events.

Patrick was standing in a corner near the bathroom, watching as the orders were being made. He had watched Brian put in his order, and Patrick had put in an order in Brian's name when he saw him come in. Patrick stood in the corner watching Boyd as he stretched his neck looking in every direction for a man that would never arrive. The hostess called out Brian's name, and Patrick stepped forward and popped the top off the cappuccino and poured a clear liquid from a vial in his pocket into the cup and put the lid down. Brian Boyd walked up as Patrick took the cup and said, "Excuse me, that cappuccino is mine." Patrick looked at him and said, "No…it's mine, slick. I ordered this before I ever saw your ass in the building." Boyd got pissed and said, "I'm a fuckin' LAPD captain. I'm on duty, and you're going to raise shit with me over my coffee?" Boyd flashed his badge with a lot of bravado. Patrick had his hand on the cup and said, "I don't give a shit if you're the fuckin' pope. It's my beverage. Wait your damn turn." Patrick released the cup as the hostess called out Brian again and put another cup on the counter. Boyd was so pissed at the response he started cursing a blue streak at Patrick.

Patrick grabbed the second cup, leaving the one he tainted for Boyd and said, "I'm sorry." Patrick picked up the cup and handed it to Boyd and said, "I didn't know you were a peace officer. I will pay for your cup of joe." He pulled out a five dollar bill, and Boyd snatched it out of his hand. "I already paid for my drink, so I will take this as your gift offer. Now, get out of my face before I find a reason to arrest you." Patrick moved up toward the front door as Boyd sipped the hot beverage looking around the restaurant. After about five minutes, Boyd had polished off the beverage and was sitting back in a corner of the shop alone away from other patrons. Patrick walked back and pulled out a chair in front of Brian's table and sat down. Brian was livid and asked, "Just who the fuck do you think you are? I told you to get your ass out of this shop and out of my sight." Patrick smiled and said, "But you're waiting for me."

Brian's face lost all color. It was a combination of the drug he had ingested in his beverage and Patrick's obvious knowledge of why he was there. "I'm waiting for who?" Brian asked with a little slur to his speech.

Patrick looked at him sitting back in the chair and said, "I believe the proper term is 'whom,' and that's Mark El Compo...right?" Brian was starting to sweat, and he tried to loosen his tie and coughed a bit and asked, "How do you know I'm waiting for Mark?" Patrick laughed. "Because Mark is unable to make it, so a friend sent me to finish you. You might have heard of him. The Iron Eagle." Boyd grabbed his chest and was having trouble breathing. Patrick stood up and walked over to him and whispered in his ear, "Vengeance is a fickle bitch, ain't it Brian? You're already dead!" Patrick turned and walked out as a woman screamed, and Boyd's body went crashing to the floor.

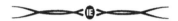

Jim and John arrived at Cantrell's home at a little before nine. The house was very, very private and sat on a corner lot. John pulled his truck around the back of the house, and he and Jim entered Garrison Cantrell's home and were greeted by the same thing Don Bartell had found the night before. They checked out the residence and found the garage and the plastic that was up. John looked on and said, "It seems Mr. Cantrell was expecting a guest." Jim had a confused look on his face and said, "Why? Because he has plastic up in his garage? Shit. Maybe he was going to paint or something." John forced out a laugh and said, "Yea...he was going to paint all right, only he was going to use blood." John pointed to a corner of the room and blood spatter that was on some boxes outside the plastic. Jim looked on and said, "Well, he's not the smartest fuck is he?" John shook his head, and they went out and got Steve's body. They placed him in the garage on the plastic. They put his service revolver in his hand with a spent shell casing on the floor at his feet, and John took a vial of blood that he had Sara draw off of Cantrell, and he spread it all around. Jim asked, "What's up with the shell casing? Steve didn't get a shot off at Cantrell?" "I checked Cantrell's wound before I left the lair. There is no bullet in his shoulder. When Charlie shot Cantrell, the bullet must have passed through." Jim got a smile on his face and said, "Ah...but Steve

and Charlie carried the same issue firearm, and the blood will confirm that Cantrell was shot with a Glock, and no one will ever find the bullet." Jim smiled sadly at Steve's body lying on the ground and said, "Steve, John is one straight-laced mother fucker, but he did good by you. You were right. He's the best damn find you ever made at the Bureau. Rest in peace, my friend." When they were finished, they drove down the street and made a 911 call that shots had been fired and waited for the police.

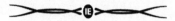

Sara, Gail, Barbara, and Jade were sitting together in the kitchen. They all had cups of coffee in front of them, but there wasn't a lot of conversation. Barbara sipped her coffee, and Jade looked at Sara and Barb and asked, "How long have you two known that John is the Iron Eagle?" Sara told her since before she married John and commenced to tell her the story of Amber, John's wife, who had been murdered, and that Walter Cruthers was her killer. Sara explained how Cruthers had abducted her as well and that the Eagle/John saved her. Barbara listened, and when Sara was done Jade asked, "And you, Barb?" "Since the night that he abducted me from my home so many years ago. I didn't know then the Eagle was John, but I knew he was a cop. I figured out John was the Eagle before he revealed his secret to me after I got to know him and Sara."

Jade took a drink of her coffee and asked, "And you two are alright with what he does as the Eagle?" Both Sara and Barbara nodded. Barbara said, "We are not just all right with it. We have helped him and will continue to until he dies, we die, or, God willing, we live to retire from this shit." Jade looked over at Gail and asked, "How long have you known?" Gail was sipping her coffee, thumbing through a magazine too relaxed. "Officially...she looked at the clock, "Less than six hours. Unofficially...Steve and I talked about it a lot over the years we were married. He suspected that John was the Eagle, but he couldn't prove it. Then after all that has happened over the past couple of years with what the Eagle and his men did to save this nation and tried to

do to save the people of Los Angeles from the fires, we both just let it be." Sara took a sip of her coffee and asked Jade, "And what about you now, Jade? You know my husband's deepest darkest secret. What are you going to do now that you're armed with this information?" The women looked on as Jade took a sip with a little shake in her hands and said, "I have always suspected that John was the Eagle. I could never put my finger on it. I just knew. There was something deep inside of me that told me he was the one behind all of these events. What am I going to do? Nothing. Not a damn thing. Am I going to help the Iron Eagle mete out justice? No...at least I don't think so. I mean...he has done so much to save so many. I've seen his brutality first hand on my autopsy table. I don't know if I could help him...I...I..."

Sara leaned over and put her hand on Jade's shaking shoulder and said, "You answered the question. We all need to shower and dress. Gail's husband is about to be found murdered in the line of duty." Gail had tears in her eyes, and she looked at Sara and said, "Last night before Steve left, he knew he wasn't coming home. We both felt it. We both had it weighing on us. He was suffering, Sara. He was losing the battle to ALS. This was his last chance to make a difference as an FBI agent." She took a deep breath and let it out, bawling, tears running down her face. "And he did it. He died the way he wanted to, protecting a fellow officer. He gave his life for the good of the people that he swore to protect." There wasn't a dry eye in the room as they broke off to shower and change.

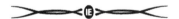

Jim and John were sitting in his pickup waiting for the call. The police were at the house and so was an ambulance. John's cell phone rang. "Swenson." There were a few moments of silence, and John said, "Give me the address, Jared, and I will pick up Sheriff O'Brian. We are on our way." He pressed the button on his phone to end the call and asked Jim, "Are you ready for this?" Jim shook his head. "Neither am I," John said as he started the truck and headed for Cantrell's home.

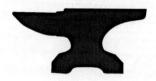

CHAPTER TWENTY-TWO

"Yea...the brain remains
conscious for up to a minute..."

The sea was flat, and there was no wind. The late morning sun was glistening off the water, and Jade sat down with her hair wet from the shower, her eyes red from crying. She sat nude, allowing the warmth of the sun to lap the remaining droplets of water from her skin until they were replaced with droplets of perspiration. She moved into the shade and sat down on a patio chair, put her head into her hands, and screamed and cried at the same time. She held the position for what seemed like hours, but it was mere seconds before she heard her cell phone ringing on the table in front of her.

She stared at the ringing phone, dreading answering it. She knew who it would be and what she would be called to do, and for the first time in her career, she doubted herself and her ability to do the job she had been elected to do. She had turned off her voicemail on the phone, so she would hear the call when it came in, and so she would be allowed the time to answer, composed. She dried her eyes and answered. Her tablet

was on the table next to her phone, and she picked it up and typed in the information. She said, "I'm en route," hung up the phone, then buried her face in her hands once more, and let out a deep primal scream of anguish and agony before dressing and heading for the crime scene.

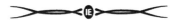

John and Jim pulled up in front of Cantrell's home. Jared was in the driveway waiting for the two men, and two FBI CSI vans were on scene as well. There were several sheriffs' deputies who were working with LAPD on keeping neighbors and onlookers back as Jim and John exited the truck. John had his FBI windbreaker on, and Jim was in his sheriff's dress uniform. Both men had showered and dressed before leaving the house with Steve's body that morning. John walked up and shook hands with Jared as did Jim, and they were getting ready to walk into the house when Jade Morgan pulled up in the coroner's car.

She got out of the car, cool and collected, and walked up to John, Jim, and Jared and said, "My CSI team is en route." They all walked into the house, which was now taped off with crime scene tape. There were two FBI cybercrime team members working on Cantrell's computers as Jared led them to the garage. "We found a spent shell casing over here, John. It's consistent with Steve's service weapon. He got a shot off. We don't know if it was before or after he was shot."

John and Jim knelt down and asked for gloves. John looked over, and Jade was with Steve's body. John took the end of a pen he had in his pocket and picked up the casing. "An evidence bag, please." He dropped the shell casing into the bag and handed it off to Jared. John said, "Where's the blood from the killer?" Jared walked the two men over and everyone parted as John and Jim worked the scene quietly together. No one dared speak, and when they were done, they walked out into the garage where Jade was working on Steve, and John asked, "Any idea on a TOD?" She looked at the thermometer that was sticking out of Steve's liver and said, "Not long. Based on my preliminary findings on scene, he was killed

between midnight and six a.m." John was standing over her and asked, "Cause of death?" Jim shot John a dirty look and said, "Well, gee, John, I'm not a coroner like Jade here, but I would say he got shot in the fuckin' chest. Seems to me to be a sure fire way to die!" John thanked him for the obvious, and Jade said, "I will give you everything as soon as I do the autopsy, and I will do it as soon as I get Steve's body back to the lab."

Jim and John worked the rest of the scene and got called to the backyard. "We got a body here!" John and Jim walked out, and one of the officers had the lid off a compost bin that Cantrell had in the backyard. There was the body of a white middle-aged male, and John looked down at his face and said, "I can ID him. The man's name is Don Bartell. He's a California Probation Officer." One of the officers working the scene asked, "What the hell would a probation officer be doing here?" Jim looked at him and said, "You don't read the fuckin' news, do you? You have your gun and badge, and you're just on the fuckin' job. Cantrell is on pretrial release for the murder of Mary Schultz, but you wouldn't know that because you're a goddamn retard. Get the fuck away from my crime scene. Go out and work the street and send one of my deputies out here who has a damn clue."

The officer walked away, and John said, "Cut them some slack." Jim fired back, "Oh, fuck no…" Jim stood up and called the officers from the outside to the kitchen of the house between the backyard and the garage and said, "Every one of you mother fuckers listen up and listen good. The bulk of you were still having your asses wiped by your mommas when Steve Hoffman and I were investigating violent crime. That man lying in there was one of my best friends. He died in the line of duty trying to protect the general public and some of you LAPD assholes from this psycho bastard. You better dot every I and cross every T in this investigation because that man in there deserves nothing less. Get educated on this killer, men, because he's out there somewhere. He may be injured, but he might very well still be alive, and by God, I want every ounce of that mother fucker's blood. Now get your asses to work."

Jade had tears in her eyes as did some of the other officers, and John walked over to Jade and whispered in her ear, "Please take care of my friend." She nodded emphatically. John said to all on scene, "Jim and I have to get back to our offices. We have a lot of people to talk to and a press conference to have about this scene. Keep your guard up, men. Cantrell is a cop killer, and he may very well still be hunting for you." Jim and John walked out of the house and got back into John's truck and drove away. John dropped Jim at his office and went on to his own to start the process of burying a hero.

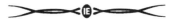

John got home at half past five. Barbara had arranged for the girls to be taken by immigration from a location in Long Beach based on John's instructions, and Sara was waiting for him when he walked in. "I saw the news conference. What you said about Steve was very touching." "Not touching, Sara. True." She nodded and asked if he was going to have dinner. He shook his head and said, "The Eagle has business to attend to. I will be late."

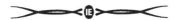

The Eagle was fast and painfully efficient when torturing Espinoza, Martel, and Rogers. He drilled out their teeth and removed their finger and toenails. While fast and efficient, it did take several days, and their cries and pleas for mercy went unheeded. They were barely breathing piles of meat when he was finished with them. The Eagle took their half dead bodies up to the property he owned on Parson's Trail in the Chatsworth Mountains and drove railroad spikes through their legs and forearms and left them nude, and still alive, for the animals to consume. The Eagle had just finished nailing Martel to two four by fours and nailing a steel cord across his throat, so he couldn't move when a pack of coyotes began to circle around the tortured remains of his victims.

The Eagle rose and said to the three, "I'm finished with you, now you can feed nature. MAY GOD NOT HAVE MERCY ON YOUR SOULS."

The Eagle walked off with a small tool kit in his hands and got into his truck. It was nearing sunset, and he sat with the windows down in the quiet of the night and heard the yelps and cries of the coyotes as they called out to others that food was to be had. He listened to the screams until they were drowned out by the savage tearing of flesh and the gurgle of blood as their throats were ripped out by the wild dogs.

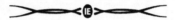

The Eagle walked into the operating room where Cantrell and El Compo were being tortured three times a day. Each time one of the men would be on the verge of death, he would bandage their wounds, feed them, and give them medication to fight off infections. As soon as they began to recover, the torture started all over again. Each man was forced to watch as the other was being torn apart by the Eagle, their flesh stripped off their bodies, each man emasculated and fed his manhood.

El Compo was branded twice daily with the very iron he used for his slaves. The Eagle recorded every torture session, getting more and more details from El Compo on his customers and his suppliers. That information was supplied to ICE as well as the FBI, the immigration department, and the Los Angeles County Sheriff's Department.

Jim put together a special taskforce whose only job was to hunt down and arrest all of the perps. In the end, nearly five hundred people were arrested, and nearly two thousand people, mostly women who had been sold into slavery, were freed from their captors and abusers. The Eagle finished El Compo in the only way he saw fit.

"Mark El Compo, you have admitted to the rape, torture, and sale of women, young female children, and men into sexual slavery. You have also admitted to torture and murder of those that you felt were either undesirable or that you tired of in your own dungeon. If a hell exists, you most certainly will go there. I, however, have worked very

hard to make your last days on this earth a hell unto itself." The Eagle uncovered the industrial meat grinder, so both men could see it. El Compo could only make noises as his teeth had been drilled then ripped out one at a time. His flesh was blistered from the repeated branding irons used on every surface of his body including his face.

El Compo's eyes had swollen shut, so he could not see what made Cantrell squeal. The Eagle took a scalpel from one of the steel tables next to El Compo's gurney and slowly cut away his eyelids and all the flesh around the eyes, exposing the eyeballs. Cantrell screamed as he watched El Compo struggle with what little strength he had and let out howls of agony as the Eagle cut away the flesh around his eyes.

The Eagle stepped back from El Compo, so he could see his fate, and he writhed and screamed against the restraints as the Eagle wrapped his wrists and moved the cherry picker over and lowered the hook and chain for the unit down to his chest. The man moved his head from side to side and looked down at the steel hook on his chest. It was impossible to make out a facial expression with his eyelids and surrounding tissue removed. El Compo could only stare as the Eagle put drops into his eyes, so they would not dry out.

The rear of the hook had been sharpened razor thin. The front of the hook, where the straps went to hold the body's weight, was solid and rounded. The Eagle turned the hook to the razor side and said, "It just isn't fair that you only got a few days of torture for all the harm and pain you caused." He slid the hook into the hole where Mark's manhood had been, and with the remote units he retracted the chain. It hooked into El Compo's pelvis, and he let out a scream as the hook slowly moved up from his pelvis through his abdomen stopping at his thorax. Blood was running out of the incised wound, and his gut was splitting open from the incision. The Eagle grabbed an oscillating saw with a rounded end and jammed it into El Compo's lower thorax and sawed through the breastbone, stopping as the blade cut through the top of the thorax. The Eagle moved the hook and with slow, steady persistence pulled the hook up the sawed incision until El Compo was split from his pelvis to his throat.

El Compo passed out a few times, but the Eagle kept giving him shots of adrenaline and stimulants that shocked him awake. "I don't want you to miss any of this, Mark. You have earned all of it," the Eagle said as he placed the hook through El Compo's wrapped hands. "I don't want to lift you off the gurney here like I would usually do. All of your innards will fall all over my floor, and I don't want that." The Eagle moved the gurney and the cherry picker over next to the meat grinder. He started the blades then took El Compo's feet in one hand and the remote for the cherry picker in the other and lifted his body high enough to be over the grinder's hopper. The Eagle slowly moved Mark's feet over the unit and yelled to El Compo over the sound of the grinder, "There. Now all of you will go into the machine." He released the legs, and El Compo swung out over the meat grinder. His midsection split from the weight of his unrestrained organs, and his intestines spilled down into the grinder.

El Compo's stare was all he had left as the Eagle slowly lowered him into the grinder. His head moved from side to side, and he tried to scream, but the pressure of the grinder and the pull of his intestines and other internal organs made it impossible.

Cantrell was doing enough screaming for the two of them as he watched El Compo disappear into the unit. The Eagle grabbed El Compo's disembodied head and held it up to Cantrell. The eyes of the skull were moving as if probing the room, and the Eagle said to Cantrell, "Believe it or not, Mr. El Compo is still alive." The Eagle pressed two fingers into the bloody spinal column of El Compo's skull, and the bodiless head winced in pain. "Yea…the brain remains conscious for up to a minute, sometimes longer."

The Eagle turned off the grinder with Mark El Compo's head in his hands and swung it around in front of Cantrell and said, "It is quite interesting to watch the undead stare into the face of its killer. He placed El Compo's head on Cantrell's chest, allowing the blood to pool. The eyes were still moving and then slowly they stopped, and the pupils began to dilate, and the Eagle said, "Well, Mr. El Compo is now dead.

Don't you worry. You will not meet such a fate. I'm going to end you by using a killing and body elimination technique I picked up from the man who killed my first wife. I'm going to need assistance, and I feel pretty strongly that Special Agent Steve Hoffman's widow will want to be involved, so we are going to make a day of it tomorrow. Do you like boats, Garrison? I guarantee you it will be one unforgettable day. There's a school of great white sharks off the Malibu coast a little over a half mile from shore, and I've been chumming the water for a week in your honor." The Eagle walked out of the operating room, leaving Garrison Cantrell screaming on the operating table.

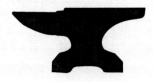

CHAPTER TWENTY-THREE

"Why does the Eagle exist?"

I t was a beautiful Saturday afternoon, and John, Jim, Sara, Gail, and Barbara had just returned to Los Angeles from Washington D.C. where a moving FBI funeral and memorial service was held for Special Agent Steve Hoffman. Steve's casket lie in state at the Hoover FBI building in Washington for three days, and then he was taken to the National Cathedral where he was memorialized in a national funeral. President Matthew Hernandez delivered a stirring and heartfelt speech about the man who he said, "Brought the plight of a nation to the government's attention."

Hernandez said, "The loss of Special Agent Steve Hoffman is not just a loss for the FBI. It's a loss for our nation. His heroics in the past several years in the face of great adversity made and kept a nation strong. In the end, Agent Hoffman made the ultimate sacrifice and was killed in the line of duty. Steve Hoffman is a hero; he is what being a member of the FBI family is about. While his death is tragic, through his death a killer of police officers was stopped, and the lives of countless others were saved. Agent Hoffman, facing

his own terminal disease battling ALS, chose to stay in the field, working alongside the men and women he once led. While Special Agent Hoffman may be gone, he will never be forgotten."

John was reading an excerpt from the president's speech as he rode in a limousine carrying him along with Gail, Jim, Barbara, and Sara to First Presbyterian Church in Santa Monica. They had flown in earlier that morning from Washington with Steve's casket, and they were on the final leg of Steve's long journey to be laid to rest beside his late wife, Molly, at Forest Lawn Cemetery in Los Angeles. The car pulled up in front of the church where the white hearse was parked with a special guard detail awaiting Steve's coffin. They exited the vehicle and saw hundreds of people lining 1220 Second Street in Santa Monica in silent reverence for a fallen officer. John looked around at the droves of people and was visibly moved.

Sara took his arm, and John took Gail's, and the three walked into the church with Barbara and Jim behind them. There were moving tributes to Steve, and both John and Jim gave brief but deeply personal eulogies as well. Jim broke down twice in his delivery, but he made it through, and as he sat back down and looked at Steve's flag draped coffin he whispered to Barbara, "If Steve could see this, he would have a shit fit!"

Jade Morgan was sitting behind them with Karen Faber. The two women were wiping away tears as the bag pipes played and Steve's casket was walked out of the church to the waiting hearse with John and Jim as pallbearers. The church was filled with every branch of law enforcement. All sat in silent reverence for their fallen comrade. When the funeral had concluded, two limousines were waiting to take family and close friends to the cemetery.

Escorted by motorcycle police from around the state and country, the hearse began its slow journey to the 101 Freeway and on to the cemetery for interment. Thousands of people lined the procession route on the way to the cemetery, many saluting as the hearse drove by. Gail wept quietly, sitting off away from the rest in the limo.

When they arrived at the cemetery, John and Jim carried Steve to his final resting place, and as they returned to their wives, Bob Zimmer, Gail's ex-husband was standing next to her, holding her hand along with his new wife, out of respect for Steve. There was a twenty-one gun salute and a quick graveside service, and the few friends threw clods of dirt on the casket before it was interred. Gail took a rose from the casket spray, smelled it, and threw it into the grave of her husband and slowly walked away.

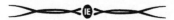

The Eagle was in with Cantrell early on Sunday morning. He had a four-by-six inch piece of pine that he had routed out and filled with molten lead. He made sure that some of it landed on Cantrell who was bloody and beaten now on the floor of the operating room with his burned hands zip tied behind his back. Sara walked in and announced, "It's nine a.m., sir." "Thank you. We will be ready in just a few minutes. Please have Gail come over." The Eagle had two horseshoe shaped objects with sharp pointed ends on them that he laid in front of Cantrell along with four eight-inch railroad spikes. He threw them down near Cantrell's body along with a twenty-pound sledgehammer.

Cantrell let out a cry, and the Eagle stood up and said, "Hold that for a moment." The Eagle left the room and walked out into the foyer where Gail was seated with Sara and Barbara. The Eagle spoke directly to Gail and asked, "I have prepared Steve's killer's final resting place, and I'm preparing to nail him to his doom. Do you wish to see him or speak to him before I begin his end?"

Gail looked up at John with an icy stare and said, "No...I want to help!" The Eagle reached out, and she took a hold of the giant hand and stood up. The Eagle went to walk her back, and she stopped and asked Sara and Barbara if they would help. They nodded, and all of them went back to Cantrell's holding room.

Cantrell saw them all walk in and was silent. The Eagle grabbed him by the back of the head and pulled him across the floor and cut

the zip ties and threw his body down on the piece of wood. Gail leaned down and put her knee into Cantrell's chest as Barbara and Sara handed the Eagle the first of the horseshoe restraints. He pounded the two spikes down into the wood, pinching Cantrell's forearms just above the wrists and affixing him to the board. He handed a spike to Gail who took it and the hammer, and he showed her where to drive it into Cantrell's arm just above the wrist.

Gail had no hesitation and drove the spikes into both wrists, smiling the whole time. Cantrell contorted in pain, and he tried to squirm with each slam of the hammer. The Eagle lifted Cantrell's nailed body over his head, and he let out a scream as the weight of his body pulled down on the nails and the restraints that affixed his body to the board.

The Eagle had two large steel posts that were mounted to the wall, and he dropped Cantrell's nailed body and board onto the protruding pieces of steel. Cantrell's feet were hanging in mid air about a foot off the floor. He was facing the wall. The Eagle took out a whip inlaid with glass and tacks and handed it to Gail. He said, "We will excuse ourselves. Come to us when you are finished with him."

Gail stood with the whip in her right hand at her side as the three exited. They stood just outside the door and listened to Gail scream obscenities at Cantrell with every strike of the whip. Cantrell's screaming made Sara and Barbara look away, and Barbara said, "My God, she's YOU!" as she looked at the Eagle. "No…she's suffering the pains of hell over Steve's death at that man's hand. She is extracting her own punishment. Do you know Gail's history?" Both Barbara and Sara nodded, and the Eagle said, "Then you understand."

Inside, Cantrell's back was looking more and more like hamburger with every strike of the whip. Blood splattered against the walls, and he had lifted his legs in defense of the whip, which only enraged Gail further. For fifteen brutal minutes, Gail beat Cantrell with the whip until she was exhausted and dripping with sweat. She took off her top and bottoms. She was wearing a bikini, and she walked up to Cantrell and whispered in his ear, "I'm going to watch you DIE while I sunbathe on the deck of the

Eagle's boat, you son of a bitch!" She wrapped the whip around Cantrell's neck and held the end of it. She slowly walked out of the room, pulling the whip with its glass and tacks around Cantrell's neck.

Once outside, with her T-shirt and shorts in hand, she said, "Well, I need a drink and some sun. Where do I meet you and your boat?" "Sara will bring you down. Give me ten minutes to get Mr. Cantrell down to the boat and situated," the Eagle said as Sara and Barbara followed Gail out of the Eagle's lair.

Sara took them back over to the main house where Jade was sitting on the sundeck with a drink in her hand, sunbathing nude. She heard the girls coming but said nothing at first. She saw Gail in her bikini and asked, "Will you be joining me?" She nodded and said, "In a few hours. I have some final business to attend to." Jade looked on at Sara and Barbara and asked, "Are you going with her?" "If she wants us to," said Sara. She had just gotten the words out when she heard Jim's voice coming through the front door. "So, is fuckin' Cantrell dead yet?"

He saw Gail and said, "I'm sorry." Gail let out a little laugh while taking off her top and bottoms and laying on a chair near Jade and asked, "For what? Cantrell is not dead yet. I just finished beating him. The Eagle is getting him to the boat, and we are going to go sunbathe while the Eagle feeds Cantrell to the sharks. Want to join us?"

Jim looked on at Sara, Barbara, and Jade. There was a moment of silence, and Sara stripped off her clothes as did Barbara, and Barbara poured them all a drink, and they laid on lounge chairs awaiting the Eagle's return. Jim looked on and said, "You can't be fuckin' serious? You're all going out with the Eagle while he murders a man?" Gail said, "It's not murder, and Cantrell is no man. This is my mourning time for Steve, and I want my friends with me, if they choose…and from the look of nude solidarity they do. Come out with us and watch the son of a bitch beg for his life while great whites nip at his feet and eat him. I understand from talking to the Eagle he has a nice unit set up to lower Cantrell ever so slowly into the water while feeding the sharks. I think it will be great fun…want to come?"

John walked back in from the lair to the living room to see all of the women nude on the sundeck. He saw Jim standing there silent and just shook his head and said, "The Eagle has made everything ready whenever you are." Gail asked, "Can the girls come, too?" John looked over at Jim who was staring longingly at the nude women on the lounge chairs in front of him. John said, "Um...yes, of course. There is plenty of room on the boat for everyone. Do you want to bring a cooler and some booze and make a party of it?" John meant it as a crude off-the-cuff remark; unfortunately for him, it wasn't taken that way.

Sara jumped up and headed for the kitchen. Jade and Gail followed, and Barbara went to the bar and pulled several different liquors and mixers along with pitchers and a couple of bags of red plastic Solo cups. Barb looked at the color of the cups and said, "Seems appropriate." She let out a laugh as she called out to the girls and said, "You might as well pack some snacks. I'm sure the Eagle is going to make this take a long time."

Jim looked at John's stunned face and said, "Seriously? You are going to have a feeding at a feeding? I mean, John, this is fucked up and twisted even by the Eagle's standards." John nodded his head slowly and said, "The Eagle is just the instrument of justice. He's not going to stand in the way of how the victim's wife and friends choose to mourn...or celebrate...or..." John stopped mid-sentence and shrugged his shoulders and walked back in the direction of the lair.

Jim called out, "That mother fucker killed one of my best friends!" John nodded, and Jim said, "When you cross that threshold, you're the Eagle, right?" John nodded. Jim asked, "I know you have to be the Eagle to mete out justice, but when you're done with Cantrell, if I'm on the boat with you, and the girls, can you be John when you're done?"

John smiled and said, "Steve's murder cleared the lines between my role as the Eagle and the agent. Yes, once I have killed Cantrell I will join in the celebration of Steve's life in any way that Gail wants to celebrate it." Jim cocked his head and said, "Does that mean you will do with Gail what Steve and Molly did with Gail?"

John laughed and said, "Are you asking me if I will have sex with Sara and Gail together if she asks?" "You're goddamn right. That's exactly what I'm asking." "How do you know that we haven't already done that?" Jim followed the Eagle into his lair all the while asking, "Have you already done that? Come on, really, seriously, have you…huh…have you?" There was silence from the Eagle, and Jim's voice was echoing off the walls of the lair as they walked out the door and down to the waiting boat with Jim repeating the question over and over again, getting no response.

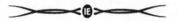

It was just after midnight, and John got out of bed and walked over to the fridge and pulled a Coke Zero out of the box and walked out onto the balcony overlooking the sea. Garrison Cantrell was dead, and it had been a long afternoon and a strange celebration. After Cantrell had been dispatched, the rest of the day on the boat had been spent with food, drink, and merriment. There had been dancing and drinking, and by the time he got the boat back to the boathouse, he had to carry all but Barbara and Jim into the house.

John laid down nude on one of the lounge chairs and cracked open the can and took a drink. He listened as the sea crashed on the shore beneath his feet, looking up at the star light. He whispered to himself, "You might be gone, Steve, but you will never be forgotten." He toasted the sky and said, "There are worse animals out there and a limited amount of time to capture them before they do more harm. The Eagle seems to be no deterrent to crime." "Yes he is," Jade whispered through the darkness.

John sat looking up at the stars as Jade came out with a drink in her hand and asked, "Is it okay if I join you?" John patted the lounge next to him, and she laid down nude on the chair. He looked over at Jade and said, "You're cold." He got up and grabbed a blanket off the back of a chair in the bedroom and gently put it over her shoulders but left the rest of her body nude in the star light. "So, what do you think, Jade? Is the Eagle a deterrent to crime?" She looked up at the

stars, taking a sip of her drink, and said, "I don't know, John. I just don't know. The Eagle works in the shadows. He's not front and center like Superman for God's sake." He nodded, taking a drink of his Coke, and said, "He's not supposed to be. That's not why he exists." Jade took a sip of her drink and turned to sit up on the lounge chair. She pulled the blanket around her shoulders and in a soft voice asked, "Why does the Eagle exist?"

"Vengeance and avenging," said Sara, walking out onto the deck nude and pulling on a robe. Jade said, "Oh God. I hope we didn't wake you?" Sara motioned to Jade for a sip of her drink, and she handed it to her. "No…I felt for my man, and he wasn't there, and when he's not in bed it means that he's off thinking, and I always interrupt him because he thinks too much."

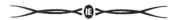

The sun was breaking the horizon, and Jim and Barbara were wrapped in each other's arms. Barbara was snoring lightly against Jim's neck as he stared up at the ceiling of their bedroom. He watched the shadow play of the morning light as the sun rose and stole the darkness. He laid in the stillness of the morning and said, "Nine more months, and I'm out of office. I better fuckin' survive it." Barbara roused and said, "You won't just survive it, you'll thrive on it." "How do you figure?" Jim said, reaching over for his cigarettes on the nightstand. He pulled one out and offered one to Barb, and she took one out of the pack. Jim flipped open his Zippo and lit the cigarettes and lay on his pillow with one hand behind his head and Barbara lying on his chest. Barbara took a hit off the smoke and rolled onto her back. Jim looked at her nude breasts and leaned over and kissed each one.

She laughed as her nipples got hard and said, "The Eagle has hardened you." He looked down at the raging erection that he had and said, "I don't get a hard on when I'm around John or the Eagle!" Barbara roared. "No, sir, you get that for me. What we all did yesterday

together to Cantrell solidified vengeance for your slain friend and also gave you a glimpse into the inner workings of the Eagle." Jim looked over at Barbara and said, "Are you saying you think that now I'm going to be a fuckin' killer like him?" She shook her head, blowing the smoke from her cigarette into the air. "No, no…I think that you and John have formed a bond over the Eagle, and you are going to have a hell of a lot harder time letting the really, really bad guys see the inside of a jail cell." Jim took a hit off his cigarette and said, "Yea…that's what I'm fuckin' afraid of, Barb, that's exactly what I'm afraid of."

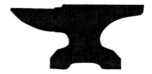

CLEANSING

The Iron Eagle Series: Book Eight

PROLOGUE

Jade Morgan ran her usual route up Topanga Canyon Road into the Malibu Hills in the Santa Monica Mountains. It was her first weekend off in nearly a month, and she needed to get out and get some air and see the light of day instead of the light of her autopsy table at the Los Angeles County Coroner's office. She ran up Topanga past the multi-million dollar homes that inhabit the private enclave in the hills overlooking Malibu and the Pacific Ocean. When she rounded the corner of her final turn before stopping for a water break, she smelled smoke.

If there is one thing that no one in Southern California ever wants to smell, it's smoke, and just the hint of it nauseated Jade. She had lived through the terrorist fires three years earlier, and the smell brought back a flood of memories. She looked around for the source but couldn't see anything. She kept running until she got to her turn and stopped. She pulled

her water bottle from a belt on her hip and took several hard breaths and sips while looking for the source of the odor. She was wiping the sweat from her brow when off in the distance of a small side trail she saw just the hint of white smoke and took off in its direction.

There were several rock caves and pits that the local kids used for their partying, and as she closed in on the source she figured that's what she had found. Only when she turned the corner and saw the source of the fire and what lay upon it, she leaned over and threw up then pounded her chest and grabbed her cell phone.

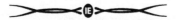

John Swenson pulled off Topanga Canyon Road where there were several sheriffs' cars parked. He got out and saw Jade off to the side talking to Jim O'Brian. She saw John walking toward them and ran into his arms, crying. He wrapped his arms around her, looking at Jim, and asked, "What the hell happened up here?" Jim waved an arm for John to follow him, and John took Jade by the hand and followed. Jim had a cigarette hanging out of his mouth, and he was in a pair of shorts and a T-shirt. John was dressed in shorts as well. They were both off work for the weekend, and it was damn early on a Saturday morning for either of them to be called out. Jade had called John, who in turn called Jim, who in turn called in the 911 to his Malibu Sheriff's office, and they had cars there before Jim and John could get on scene.

John had Jade by the hand, and she walked silently by his side, following Jim down a slight embankment until they came to a rock wall and the remnants of a fire. John looked on and said, "Okay…so some kids were up here having a party and a cook out!" Jim pointed in the direction of the smoldering fire and said, "Well, then we have a bunch of mother fuckers up here who eat babies!" John looked down to see the half burned corpse of a child. It had been skewered through the bottom with the pointed end protruding through its skull. Half of the child was unidentifiable. The face was somewhat discernible,

and John left Jade behind him and said, "It's been eaten…or part of it has." Jim looked on saying, "Well, no fuckin' shit, Sherlock. Nothin' gets past you, does it?"

John looked at Jade and said, "I know this is traumatic, Jade, but I need you to do your job. She dried the tears from her face and took a deep breath and walked over to the crime scene. She said, "Um…looks to be male. Based on his size, I would say between one and five months old. Um…there are some teeth marks on the victim. They appear to be animal bites, maybe coyote or some other scavenger. I will need to get him on the table to know more." She stood up and looked over at Jim who was staring at something. John looked over at Jim as well and asked, "Jim, did you hear any of what Jade just said?" "Yea…I heard every mother fuckin' word…I have a feeling this is only the beginning of something a hell of a lot more terrifying."

He pointed with his right hand, a cigarette between his fingers, at a rock wall behind where the body was located. John and Jade came around and looked to see an inscription chiseled into the rock. Jim said, "This took a lot of time to do, guys. This is not some street artist. This is something way freakier." John looked on and read the inscription out loud.

"PSALM 26

"VINDICATE ME, O LORD,
FOR I HAVE WALKED IN MY INTEGRITY.
I HAVE ALSO TRUSTED IN THE LORD;
I SHALL NOT SLIP.
EXAMINE ME, O LORD, AND PROVE ME;
TRY MY MIND AND MY HEART.
FOR YOUR LOVING KINDNESS IS BEFORE MY EYES,
AND I HAVE WALKED IN YOUR TRUTH.
I HAVE NOT SAT WITH IDOLATROUS MORTALS,

NOR WILL I GO IN WITH HYPOCRITES.
I HAVE HATED THE ASSEMBLY OF EVILDOERS,
AND WILL NOT SIT WITH THE WICKED.
I WILL WASH MY HANDS IN INNOCENCE;
SO I WILL GO ABOUT YOUR ALTAR, O LORD,
THAT I MAY PROCLAIM WITH THE VOICE OF
THANKSGIVING,
AND TELL OF ALL YOUR WONDROUS WORKS."
NKJV

Jim and Jade looked on at John as he read, and when he had finished Jim said, "I don't know about you two, but I think unholy fuckin' shit about covers it." John looked at the wall and said, "You're not kidding, Jim. Someone took a hell of a lot of time and even cited the version of the bible this was taken from." Jade looked on and asked, "What does it mean?" John and Jim looked at each other, and Jim said, "Big trouble, that's what it means, Jade, big mother fuckin' trouble."

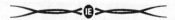

The smiling face of the young woman at the front door of the house on San Jose Street in Granada Hills was full of excitement. Emily Robinson had owned the home in the upper middle class neighborhood for thirty years. She was pleasant but firm with the girl. "Thank you for stopping by, young lady, but whatever you're selling I'm certain I already have it." "No ma'am. I am a hundred percent certain that you don't have what I'm offering." The young woman had a bible in her hand and dead eyes. Emily knew what she was selling, and she wasn't interested. Her grandson, Robert, came walking up to the door and asked, "Who's dat, granny?" Robert was small for his age. At one, he was only about the size of a six-month old. He walked with a slight limp, and the girl greeted him enthusiastically.

"My name is Lisa. Lisa Farmer. What's your name?" Her smile lit up the dimly lit foyer, and he said "Robert!" proudly. Lisa reached her hand in and took Robert's hand and shook it gently and said, "It's nice to meet you, Robert." Emily had had enough and said, "Thank you but no thank you. Now, if you don't mind, I have grandchildren to feed." Lisa started to say something, but the door slammed in her face. She walked back out to the street where a white windowed van was parked. The driver got out and asked, "Did you deliver the good news?" Lisa looked at the ground and said, "She wouldn't listen." The man put his hand on her shoulder and said, "Not everyone will, Lisa, not everyone will. Did you talk to anyone else at the house?" She nodded and said, "A little boy named Robert. He was very sweet." The man smiled and said, "Well, the Lord works in mysterious ways. Perhaps the Lord will work through Robert." Lisa got into the van, and the driver closed the door. He jotted down the address and then got into the van and drove off down the street.

He called back to Lisa and asked, "Do you think that Robert would come to you if you called him?" "Yes, pastor, I do." "Good, good. That's enough for today. I will take you all back to the house." The driver smiled and began singing a hymn. The others joined in. He held the steering wheel tight between his fingers and said to himself quietly, "I heard you slam the door on God there, Grandma. You have dipped your hands in muddy water and through God the Father I shall make you clean."

About the Author

Roy A Teel Jr. is the author of several books, both nonfiction and fiction. He became disabled due to Progressive Multiple Sclerosis in 2011 and lives in Lake Arrowhead, CA with his wife, Tracy, their tabby cat, Oscar, and their Springer Spaniel, Sandy.

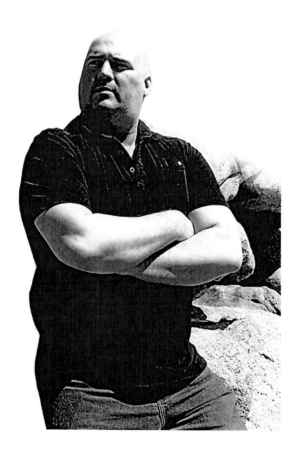

CPSIA information can be obtained at www.ICGtesting.com
Printed in the USA
BVOW05*0736200316

440993BV00001B/4/P